TWIN TERROR

TWIN TERROR

Good Seed, Bad Seed
A Thriller from the World of Consciousness

JAMES A. CUSUMANO

WATERFRONT PRESS

This series of novellas is dedicated to two special friends—Deepak Chopra, who showed me the power of mindfulness and spirit, and Rinaldo Brutoco, who through his creative efforts at the World Business Academy, has demonstrated how technology and business linked to mindfulness and spirit can elevate global social consciousness. Working together, these two giants continue to design a path to better humanity and create a sustainable future.

ACKNOWLEDGMENTS

Drafts of this novella were read and critiqued by my wife Inez, my daughter Polly Cole, and my sister Camille Cusumano—an accomplished author in her own right. I am deeply grateful to each of them for their valuable and constructive commentary.

Contents

THIS SERIES

"He who looks outside, dreams; He who looks within, awakens."
—Carl Jung

Twin Terror is the second novella in a series that weaves together fictional stories with meaningful concepts from metaphysics, mindfulness, science and technology. Each novella addresses controversial and hopefully, stimulating subjects, in a straight-forward, non-technical manner that can be read in less than two hours at average reading speed—a kind of "small book for short flights!"

Twin Terror is a fictional thriller that taps into the power of *Cosmic Consciousness* as well as mindfulness and Eastern Wisdom concepts as a means to explore and explain tragic events that befall the two protagonists, identical twins Sally and Sandra Brunel. The story tells of them, their family, and friends on a journey that finally leads to unexpected redemption and resolution.

Future novellas will treat subjects such as hypnosis, remote viewing, distant celestial worlds, the optimal ratio of feminine-to-masculine energies, extraterrestrials, instantaneous induction of higher levels of consciousness in multitudes of people, and a new world order, among others. All are set in a thriller genre.

The primary objective in taking this approach is to stimulate and stretch the thinking of the reader concerning the real and potential impact of consciousness and mindfulness in our lives thus moving us above and beyond so-called *well-proven, logical* concepts.

Enjoy your read!

James A. Cusumano
Prague
February 2017
www.JamesCusumano.com

DISCLAIMER

This book is a work of fiction. Many of the names, characters, places and incidents in this book are products of the author's imagination. Historical, religious or mythological characters and events and places are used fictitiously. Any resemblance to any actual persons, living or dead, past events or historical locations, is entirely coincidental. While some notable persons, places and concepts are not fictitious, attempts have been made to blend references to them seamlessly with those of fictitious persons, places and concepts strictly for the purpose of the reader's enjoyment.

PROLOGUE

*"I do not fear death. I had been dead for billions
and billions of years before I was born, and had not
suffered the slightest inconvenience from it."*
—Mark Twain

Have you ever wondered what it would be like to die? I'm sure you have at one time or another. We all do. Well, I can tell you it's one of the most incredible experiences you could ever imagine.

If you really think about it, most of us live our day-to-day lives as if we were immortal. I guess if we didn't, the incredible fear and stress of constantly anticipating our last day would mount so rapidly that all would likely be over in a flash.

I certainly lived one of those *normal immortal* lives. I had no idea the *Grim Reaper* would visit me just before my 16th birthday. *Sandra Brunel, it's your time.*

His message was beyond disconcerting. My life was just beginning to move from mad mayhem to a productive rewarding future. Most important to me, my twin sister, Sally, and I finally worked out our years of personal differences and learned to accept and intelligently manage the paranormal gifts we were born with.

But *Cosmic Consciousness*, God or whatever label you choose to call the *One* that is within and without every one of us, oversees a much bigger picture than any of us are capable of uncovering in a single lifetime. And when your time arrives, it's in the best interest of the entire Universe, as well as yours.

One consequence of my current state of "existence" is that I can share with you completely, accurately and without prejudice or personal bias exactly how the lives in our family unfolded and their impact on my demise. I am now directly connected to the *Akashic Field of Consciousness*, sometimes called the Akashic Records, the Universe's complete memory of every thought, event, and emotion that has ever occurred. It's all encoded in a non-physical plane of existence known as the *Astral Plane*, the world of *celestial spheres* traveled by the soul on its way through birth, death, rebirth and the same continuum for as long as is necessary for each and every individual to reach what some might call *enlightenment*.

I learned so much during those 16 years. I have since thought over and over that *I would do so many things differently, if I had a chance for a second try.*

It now appears I will have that opportunity.

Chapter 1
The Wish

"Be careful what you wish for!"
—Chinese Proverb

Mom and Dad were hard-working professionals. Dad was a sales representative for a multinational pharmaceutical firm and Mom was head of human resources for a software company in Santa Barbara. Despite the intensity of their respective professional commitments, there was nothing they wanted more in their lives than their first child.

But, the results were not as they had hoped. Mom, not inherently a religious or spiritual person, found herself daily imploring the forces of the universe to "please deliver" them a child.

When Nature's way did not respond favorably after five years of marriage, they did what many modern couples in their situation do. They sought the help of the best *in-vitro* clinic where they lived in Santa Barbara.

It was an emotional challenge. But they soldiered on and then two years later—finally, success! At least that's how it all began.

As Sally's *older* sister, I entered this world on April 14, 2001, three and one-half minutes before her. From that first moment, I was without question, considered the dominant twin. I was physically active. And I demanded lots of attention—mostly I got it too, if only to turn off my ruckus and screams of discontent.

Sally, on the other hand, was docile and contemplative from the moment she saw the light of this world. She looked about the room, taking in the new forms and figures in her amazing new environment. *The darkness was gone!*

Although Mom and Dad had not anticipated twins, they were exhilarated and adapted with some outside help to the daily challenge of raising two babies simultaneously. They adored our shiny blond hair, piercing green eyes and what our pediatrician said were as perfectly shaped anatomies as could be expected for infants. It looked like the four of us Brunels were at the beginning of what would be the perfect American family.

As our lives unfolded over the next 16 years, no one could have predicted the terror that would be inflicted upon our family. And I was totally to blame.

Chapter 2
The Decision

"Quick decisions are unsafe decisions."
—Sophocles

Whether or not it was malfeasance in applying the *in-vitro* technology was impossible to know. But the first challenge occurred one week after Sally and I were born. Sally was rushed to the hospital with a high temperature and what appeared to be the onset of a deadly sepsis infection.

After several blood and urine tests, it was determined that her right kidney was not only non-functional, but was infected with a rare bacterial agent that threatened to spread throughout her entire body and shut down all her internal organs. The doctors had no idea as to the source of the infection. However, they plowed forward urgently trying to discover the key to saving my sister's life.

She underwent immediate surgery to remove the infected non-functioning kidney. Then three weeks later, after near continuous intravenous infusions of *ampicillin* and *gentamicin,* she was a bit weak and under weight, but generally healthy again, and was discharged from the hospital. Sally's challenge foreshadowed much of what was to come in our lives together over the next 16 years. Just like it's better not to know your final day of reckoning, it's also best not to have any inkling of the physical and emotional challenges you will face in the future.

However, it was only a few months after birth that Sally and I were seen by our doctors as being different and unusual, although Mom and especially Dad seemed oblivious to their comments. We had already shown signs of well-above normal behavior physically, mentally and emotionally. And those advances would only accelerate with time.

Shortly after our third birthday, Mom and Dad finally came to grips with their, and our doctors', observations over the prior three years. It was the result of an argument.

"Margaret, for God's sake, there is nothing wrong with them! They're just a bit advanced for their age."

"Alan, please let's try to look at this as objectively as we can."

"I am, and I don't see a problem."

"No problem? Then tell me this, why is it that they were both walking at six months? And speaking like three-year-olds before their first birthday? But most significantly, and certainly most frightening to me, how is it that they both seem to know when and who is approaching from another room?"

"Margaret, it's coincidence, I assure you."

"Coincidence? Alan, just two days ago you left for work and 20 minutes later, Sally was saying, 'Daddy's coming home.' I assured her you were on your way to work. Less than a minute later, you were barging through the front door, concerned about finding your office keys which you thought you had left in the bathroom.

"While you rummaged unsuccessfully through the bathroom, Sally walked into the den and recovered your office keys. They had fallen behind the TV. You probably would have never found them!

"Alan, this is not normal! And you know this is just one example of many. I'm concerned as to what it means. Dr. Ryan said we should see a child psychologist."

"Okay, okay, I tell you what. I will set up an appointment for the girls to see Dr. Martin Zang."

"Who's he?"

"He has his practice over in Ojai. You remember I told you about him. He gave an incredible lecture in San Francisco at last year's annual conference on *The Impact of Epigenetics on the Future of Healthcare*. He is most unusual because he is not only a practitioner of Chinese medicine, but also received his medical degrees in both allopathic and homeopathic medicine in the U.S. And if that's not enough, he has a PhD in child psychology from Harvard!"

Mom exhaled deeply. "Honey that would please me to no end. Let's do it!"

Dad caressed Mom. As usual in their disagreements, they had reached a mutually acceptable decision. But it was only the beginning.

CHAPTER 3
BEGINNINGS

"There is nothing either good or bad, but thinking makes it so."
—Shakespeare

Good ole' Dr. Zang; oh boy, did I give him the runaround. He really didn't deserve it. He was just trying to help Sally and me. But as usual, my desire for personal control and general disrespect for authority got the best of me.

He had a beautiful office in a multi-million dollar historical mansion, located on McNell Road in Ojai's quiet, posh, East End. A dedicated holistic practitioner, he moved to Ojai some years ago from Los Angeles, yearning for a more spiritual and healthy environment. Not surprising he chose Ojai; it's located in a magical valley, just across the Santa Ynez Mountains from Santa Barbara, and a 20-minute drive inland from the city of Ventura on the coast. It's covered with avocado, orange and citrus orchards, and in April and May, the floral aroma from the orange groves is magnificently intoxicating.

Surrounded by striking 5,000-foot mountains, Ojai is affectionately known by its nickname *Shangrila*. Spiritualists maintain it is located on one of three of the world's highest energy vortices. Many people claim they experience this energy, especially on Mediation Mountain, located a stone's throw from Dr. Zang's office. I guess it's no surprise that Jiddu Krishnamurti, one of the highly-recognized spiritual and philosophical figures of the 20th century created his foundation in Ojai, where it operates to this day.

Dr. Zang had no challenge attracting well-heeled clients with his impeccable academic pedigree and credentials. It also did not hurt that the Ojai Valley was home to some of the wealthiest in the movie industry. Reese Witherspoon, Diane Ladd, Johnny Cash, Jake Gyllenhaal, Larry Hagman, Anthony Hopkins, Malcolm McDowell, Bill Paxton, Mary Steenburgen, Tim Burton and many more live or have lived there. It was much before my time, but as I understand it, this artsy village of some 8,000 people is probably best known to baby boomers as the filming location for *The Six Million Dollar Man* and *The Bionic Woman* TV series in the mid to late 1970s, but more practically, for the internationally-recognized and luxurious Ojai Valley Inn & Spa. On weekends, it's filled to the brim with the *Who's Who* from the film industry.

It was to this setting that Mom and Dad made the 30-minute drive twice a week so that Dr. Zang could conduct an extensive battery of psychological and physical tests on Sally and me. After several weeks, a conference was set with Mom and Dad to discuss his findings. They left us at home with our long-time babysitter, Sharon Levinson. As Mom and Dad waited for Dr. Zang in the reception area, they were clearly anxious about their meeting. Even Dad, who maintained there were no issues with us, was tapping his foot and fidgeting with his fingers.

Dr. Zang entered the room and greeted Mom and Dad in his usual pleasant, relaxed manner. "Good evening Margaret and Alan. Please come into my office."

Dad stammered just a bit, "We sure are anxious to understand what you've found."

"I understand, Alan. My findings are somewhat complex, but I will do my best to help you understand them."

Without skipping a beat, Mom reacted, "Oh my God is there a major problem?"

"No Margaret, nothing like that. But there are some important challenges, and I want to be frank with you about them and be sure you both understand what they are. Managed properly, they could provide significant benefits to the girls."

Mom and Dad sat their quietly, but with obvious apprehension.

"First of all, absent the fact that Sally is running on one kidney, both children are physically very healthy. In fact, I doubt they could be any healthier!"

"Well, that's fantastic! See Margaret, what did I tell you? They're just fine."

"Now Alan, don't jump the gun, there is much more to discuss."

"Sorry. Please proceed."

Mom squeezed Dad's hand. She was worried.

"Having quickly found them to be physically healthy, I spent essentially 90 percent of my time testing their psychological and emotional characteristics. As you might imagine, it's complicated to do this with three-year-olds. But I'm sure you both understand that Sally and Sandra are well beyond their years in intelligence. In fact, on that score, Sandra has an IQ of 175 and Sally's is 185. For comparison, Albert Einstein's has been estimated at 160. Your children both measure well above the genius category, which can be both a good thing and a challenge."

Mom responded inquisitively, "We knew they were clever, but had no idea that their IQ was that high. They're geniuses?"

"Their IQ is not my primary concern. I think with good counsel that can be managed through their youth and into adulthood. There has been a lot of good research in this area. What causes me greater concern is that both children appear to have other "gifts," if I may call them that. They are best known as paranormal traits, and from what I have observed so far, include telepathy, remote viewing, and amazingly even *telekinesis*."

Mom asked, "What in the world is *telekinesis*?"

"They can move material things with their thoughts."

Dad's was greatly surprised. "Are you kidding me?"

"No, I'm not. Allow me to show you a video of one of the tests I gave them."

Dr. Zang turned on a video in his computer. "I showed both girls a compass needle and how it consistently points in the northerly direction, which they both assured me, they already knew. I then showed Sandra this simple device which looks like a compass, but is not a compass. As you can see, it's simply a pin attached perpendicularly to the center of a small board, and balanced on the tip of the pin there is a thin free-floating metal arrow very similar to that on a compass. Sandra confided that her favorite treat is Gummy Bears, so I told her if she looked at the needle and could get it to move I would give her a bag of Gummy Bears. Here is the result."

As they watched Sandra focus in the video, it was only a few seconds before the needle completed a nearly 180-degree turn. Mom and Dad were in shock. They thought it must be some kind of trick. But they knew Dr. Zang was a serious man.

"But that's not the end of it. Look at what Sally can do. Not surprising, her favorite treat was also Gummy Bears. I won't even show you the results for the pin wheel, which is much easier to rotate than the compass needle because the compass needle must overcome the attractive force of the earth's magnetic field. So just look at this compass."

As they observed Sally staring at the compass face, the needle overcame the magnetic force field that naturally guides the needle in a northerly direction. The needle instead continuously turned 360 degrees over and over again.

Mom was flabbergasted and didn't know what to say. Dad spoke first in a subdued and frightened tone. "Dr. Zang, what does all of this mean?"

"Look, Alan, Margaret, there have been numerous anecdotal reports over the ages of telekinesis, levitation, telepathy and other so-called supernatural or paranormal phenomena. Few of these reports have been properly documented. Many may well be hoaxes. However, I can tell you from my personal experience in Asia, these capabilities do exist. The fact is that contemporary scientists cannot explain such phenomena with our current knowledge of physics, and even if they tried, they would most likely be rejected as quacks by their peers.

"These phenomena are beyond the principles and laws of classical Newtonian physics and in most instances, even unexplainable by the laws of modern quantum physics. Some forward-looking scientists, who believe me, have endured their share of deep criticism, think that these phenomena can only be explained by the next evolution of physics, something they call *Spiritual Physics*. But I won't even try to defend them or explain the details of this field of endeavor. It is well beyond my expertise. What I can say is that paranormal studies have quietly taken place over the years at more than a dozen major U.S. universities such as Duke and Princeton, and these powers seem to be related to a person's innate capability to access higher levels of consciousness.

"It means that your daughters both have what most would consider supernatural gifts—off-the-chart high IQ, telepathy, remote viewing, telekinesis, and who knows what else? In this country, practitioners sometimes label children like Sally and Sandra as *Indigo Children*, but I believe that's just a catch-all phrase for gifted children. You will need counsel as they mature. I am not sure who can help you, but I will try to find someone.

"Oh, and there is one more point I would like to make. I found Sandra to show excessive sibling rivalry towards Sally. For example, when she saw what Sally could do with the compass needle, she demanded to be retested. To appease her, I let her repeat the test. But when she could not accomplish nearly what Sally did, she shoved the compass off the table on to the floor and insisted that I had controlled the results."

Yes, I did do that. It was another example of my temper and ego out of control. But I would have much more than the compass incident to regret before my 16 years were up. Mom and Dad took this all in, but they were so stunned by what they heard that Dr. Zang's comment about me just seemed to float right past them. On one hand, they had two incredibly bright daughters. But on the other, their so-called "gifts" were frightening, and certainly if not properly used could be dangerous to us and to others.

CHAPTER 4
EARLY SIGNS

"I never think of the future. It comes too soon."
—Albert Einstein

Even at 10 years of age, Sally was quite adept at letting me think I was the winner whenever we had a disagreement. In retrospect, I can now see there were two reasons for this. First, she was afraid of my physical strength and that I was always manically driven to win, *no matter what*. Sally knew better than to let things come to blows. And second, it's now very clear that she far surpassed me not only in IQ, but in EQ—emotional intelligence—as well. She was always confident she could eventually manage any of our arguments in a way that didn't matter to me—except for that one unfortunate time.

It was a balmy Friday afternoon and Sharon was "child-sitting" us as usual, my sense of superiority detested the word "babysitting." Sharon had been with us since we were four years old and I must admit, she was quite good at managing nearly all of our behaviors stemming from our advanced intelligence and paranormal capabilities. For the most part, Sally and I loved and listened to her. She was cute, patient, non-threatening and knew how to adjust her ideas of play to satisfy both of us.

Because it was the beginning of a busy social weekend, Sharon was hoping that either Mom or Dad would leave work early that day so she could race home for a quick shower and a change of clothes before her date that evening with her boyfriend Marcel.

It was 4:30 pm and we were playing upstairs, quietly as usual. I was kneeling on the floor of my bedroom intensely focused on completing a Lego project I had designed. It was a sprawling and intricate sci-fi city, engaged in warfare between its planetary inhabitants and an invading force from the planet MC2 in the Andromeda constellation, at least that's how I explained it to Sharon. Sally was lying on my bed reading Anne Frank's *The Diary of a Young Girl*.

Sharon, a relatively simple but reliable 18-year-old, took our high-intellectual output very much in stride, even though we already spoke then with the presence and vocabulary of girls in their late teens. She was so adapted to the rapid evolution of our apparent unique abilities that nothing we said or did fazed her. She just thought of us as two super-bright 10 year-olds. I guess that's why we got along so well, even when I was in one of my snotty moods, which, unfortunately, was quite often.

"Okay girls, I'm going downstairs to make you a snack to hold you over until dinner. It looks like your mom and dad will be a bit late this evening, and so will dinner. Please call me on the intercom if you need me. I'll be back in about 15 minutes."

"Fine, Sharon," I responded, dispassionately.

Sally added, "Sharon, would you be so kind as to chop up some veggies, julienne style with sour cream dip; you know, the way you did last week? They are so yummy, and healthy too."

I couldn't help myself, "Sally, why are you so focused all the time on eating healthy? Just because you have one kidney doesn't mean you have to live a vegetarian existence!"

"Come on Sandra, it has nothing to do with my lone kidney. Why not eat something that's good for you, especially if it tastes good?"

"Whatever."

"Now girls, it's certainly not worth arguing over snacks. You can both have something you each like, as long as it's reasonably healthy. So, what about you Sandra? What would you like?"

It was clearly one of my bad days: "A grilled-cheese sandwich with rye bread and brie, and bring it up here while it's hot. I don't like it when the cheese gets cold."

"Well, aren't you the testy one today? Did you get up on the wrong side of the bed, little Sandra?"

"No, I did not Sharon! And my name is Sandra. You can forget the 'little.' How would you like it if I called you 'big' Sharon?"

Sharon stared at me for a few seconds and I guess decided not to retaliate. She knew when I was in one of my moods, it was a useless exercise. She also knew she could never outwit me, even at my tender age of 10. What a brat I could be!

Sharon turned on her heels and headed downstairs to the kitchen, leaving Sally and me to carry on.

"Sandra, have you ever heard of Anne Frank?"

"Of course, do you think I'm lame? Everyone with half a brain knows her story. Why?"

"Well, what amazes me is that at the age of 13, she knew exactly what her life purpose was. Listen to this."

"Oh Sally, please spare me, will you?"

"Come on Sandra, just one minute. Please."

"Fine."

"In her diary she writes:

I finally realized that I must do my schoolwork to keep from being ignorant, to get on in life, to become a journalist, because that's what I want! I know I can write…

I want to be useful or bring enjoyment to all people, even those I've never met. I want to go on living even after my death! And that's why I'm so grateful to God for having given me this gift, which I can use to develop myself and to express all that's inside me!

When I write I can shake off all my cares. My sorrow disappears, my spirits are revived! But, and that's a big question, will I ever be able to write something great, will I ever become a journalist or a writer?

"Isn't that amazing, Sandra. She knew exactly what she would do for the rest of her life!"

"Yeah, amazing, considering she just had another three years to live."

"I know. That's the sad part. I think she would have been among the great writers of our time had she lived. Just look at the success she has had with the only book she ever wrote—and at the age of 13! She apparently died in a concentration camp of typhus. It's almost as if she knew she would die and wanted to inspire people in the future with her diary—*I want to go on living even after my death!*"

"So what's your point?"

"Well, everyone tells us we're gifted children, but what good is it if you don't know where to use your gifts? I wish I knew what I would be excited to do when I grow up—just like Anne Frank knew."

"You have another three years until you're 13, so why worry?"

"Honestly, Sandra, you never seem to see my point of view. I'm not asking you to agree with it, but at least say you understand my concern."

Building on Sharon's dig, I retaliated, "Don't be so sensitive 'little' sister!"

With that, in one of her rare moments of anger and distress, Sally got up and tossed her book on to the end table next to my bed. Unfortunately, in her dismay, she heaved it a bit too hard and it flew off the table and landed on my Lego creation at the perfect spot to demolish half of my space city.

I stood up and was furious, completely out of control. "Look what you've done, and you did it on purpose!"

"I'm sorry Sandra, I didn't mean to do that. I'll help you fix it."

"No! Don't touch anything!"

"Fine, then. I'm going downstairs to have my snack."

I was fuming. I followed Sally at close range to the top of the stairs. "I want to know why you threw your book and destroyed my space city."

"Sandra, I told you I didn't mean it, and I'm sorry. I will help you rebuild it if you let me."

"Sure, then it's your city as well. Right 'little' sister?"

"No, not at all!"

I can't explain what came over me; I began to poke Sally in the chest. "I know your manipulative ways. You do it all the time. You think I don't see it? Well you're wrong! *Let Sandra think she's won* while you get your way in the long run. I know your tactics."

At that point, we were both standing on the top step leading downstairs. In a fit of rage, I poked her a little too hard and Sally went tumbling down the stairs. She screamed and reached out with both arms arresting her fall halfway down the stairs.

She began to cry. "My arm! My arm!"

I stood at the top of the stairs and made no attempt to approach her with even a semblance of sympathy. I wanted to, but I couldn't. I simultaneously felt, *she deserves the fall*, and *oh my God, what have I done*? In those seconds I saw for the first time a *bad seed* present in my soul, and I was deeply frightened yet otherwise emotionally paralyzed.

Sharon, having heard the commotion came running around to the stairwell.

"Oh my God, what happened?"

My immediate dispassionate response was, "She slipped."

Sharon picked up Sally and carried her down to lie on the living room sofa.

"Sally, where does it hurt?"

"My wrist feels terrible."

"What happened?"

By this time I was standing immediately next to Sally as she lay on the sofa. Both of us stared at each other. Our crystal clear green eyes were mutually engaged with laser-like focus. We were both frightened and speechless for different reasons; both on opposite sides of the same coin.

"I guess I slipped on the top stair. It'll be fine Sharon. I think it's just a slight sprain." Sally stood up from the sofa and put her arm around Sharon and stared at me.

I managed a slight smile and walked back upstairs to repair my Lego space city.

Sharon looked at me as I walked away and slowly climbed the stairs, not losing her gaze until I disappeared from view.

CHAPTER 5
THE INCIDENT

"Nothing is easier than to denounce the evildoer;
nothing is more difficult than to understand him."
—Fyodor Dostoyevsky

Mom and Dad had great difficulty fully accepting and acknowledging Sally's and my advanced intelligence and unusual capabilities. They also discounted the continuous stress and strain between the two of us as ordinary sibling rivalry. They wanted us to be and act like "normal" children and grow up doing the kinds of things most kids do. Thus, it was no surprise they chose the conventional education route and placed us in the Santa Barbara public school system. The school we attended was advanced by most standards and the administration tried their best with us. But they had never matriculated students like Sally and me, and in the end, we were quite miserable. It was a strain for the whole family. After all, as seven-year olds we had skipped grades one through five and started our education in middle school at grade six.

The three years to grade nine were increasingly torturous for us. We had no friends and were considered freaks by most of the students in our classes. We consistently knew the answers to nearly every question well before any of the other students, and could solve advanced algebraic equations faster than our math teacher.

But Mom and Dad saw some light at the end of this dark tunnel—or so they thought.

Dr. Zang had introduced them to Allison Bryan. Allison was an experienced and visionary educator well beyond the best in her field. She had her choice of any private school in the U.S. She chose The Thatcher School in Ojai, considered to be one of the top 10 private boarding schools in North America. After 15 successful years, and much to the dismay of the Thatcher administration, she decided it was time to follow her ultimate dream.

So she started a school in Ojai exclusively dedicated to highly-gifted children. Over the years at Thatcher, and while on sabbaticals, she had developed the details for a concept she was confident could address the needs of genius children without subjecting them to the social challenges they would face in a traditional school environment. At Thatcher, as was the case for Sally and me in the Santa Barbara system, the norm was to determine the child's IQ and then place the student in the "appropriate" grade. Unfortunately, for highly gifted children, this often meant, as Mom and Dad painfully discovered, placing Sally and me as 10-year-olds in a high school class surrounded by teens facing the usual emotional challenges of sexual confusion, drinking and search for personal identity. As you might imagine, that just didn't work well for us.

Allison's *Wisdom Academy* was supported by a hefty MacArthur Genius Grant and substantial financing from an anonymous billionaire donor she had met as the parent of one of her student's during her tenure at The Thatcher School. With this kind of support and an inspiring strategic plan, she was able to attract the best and brightest of highly competent and dedicated teachers from an international roster.

At Wisdom Academy, the children were taught in a format not unlike the old classic "one-room school house." The curriculum had certain elements of the classical Socratic method; it was designed so that students learned not only from teachers, but also from each other. There were three specially designed "Wisdom Rooms" in the school and students, ranging in age from five to 14, were changed around within these three rooms on a semiannual basis. The physical set-up and acoustical design was such that three complementary-skilled teachers could readily function simultane-ously within a Wisdom Room, causing no distraction among the other groups. After only a few years of operation, Wisdom Academy was working so well that it had attracted significant international attention with representation from 12 countries among the student body of twenty-four geniuses. Accolades in a Time Magazine article on education certainly helped.

After extensive written and oral testing, Sally and I were accepted to the school. The hefty annual non-boarding tuition of $30,000 per student was offset by some financial aid Mom and Dad were able to manage with the assistance of Dr. Zang. However, there were other not-insignificant expenses such as Bruce, our nearly full-time driver who escorted us to school from Santa Barbara and then picked us up after classes and any after-school activities. There were also several costly international trips we took during the year as part of the learning curriculum. All in all, it was a bit of a financial burden for our family, but Mom and Dad were able to manage it. It was the only reasonable way forward for us if we were to hopefully flourish in this world.

Sally and I were doing well at Wisdom Academy; that is until the incident with Maximilian Shen. Max was a bright, but troubled eight-year-old from Thailand. His wealthy parents were in the import-export business of luxury goods, so he rarely saw them. He was essentially raised by a combination of a live-in *au pair* and his aging maternal grandmother. Although his IQ was off the charts, Max suffered from ADHD and Asperger syn-drome. He was constantly fidgeting and was quite susceptible to engaging in daring, fantastical feats to demonstrate his worth and superiority.

During the first week of school, on a dare from one of our classmates, Max snuck out of his dorm room one evening with a flashlight, clothed only in pajamas, a bathrobe and slippers, and attempted to climb Chief Peak, at 5,587 feet, the highest moun-tain in the Ojai Valley. Entrance to the hiking path was located just behind the school.

Unfortunately, a third of the way up to the top, he came face-to-face with a large mountain lion. Max managed to quickly climb a nearby tree, knowing full well the cat could easily follow him up there if he chose to do so. But fortunately, the lion either wasn't that hungry, or didn't like the looks of Max and went on his merry way.

Early that morning, after a classmate contacted a school official with his concerns about Max's safety after realizing he had not returned to his room that night, a rescue helicopter pilot spotted Max clinging precariously to the top branch of the tree. In any other school he would have been expelled, but not at Wisdom Academy. He underwent a battery of psychological tests and was given counseling on how to deal with foolish and dangerous dares from others. If only it had sunk into his intelligent but troubled mind.

I'll be honest, like many of my classmates I disliked Max from the very start. I saw him as a bumbling show-off and avoided him like the plague. Plus, he was much smarter than me, and at the time, with my soaring ego, I found Max unbearable. But Sally felt sorry for him because of the teasing he faced from others in class. It was also obvious that Max enjoyed Sally's authentic compassion and they often spoke and played together. Despite their friendship, he clearly disliked me and I knew it, but at the time I could care less.

One afternoon, our lunch break took place in a beautiful arbor in the exterior school atrium, surrounded by ancient wild oaks. While students munched on avocado and mixed veggie sandwiches and sipped on a specially formulated, tasty, green juice, our science instructor, Miss Meagan, gave a non-technical lecture on the emerging field of epigenetics—how nurture and the environment very often trumps nature.

Essentially, epigenetics maintains that your environment can be as important and often more important than your genetic makeup in determining your physical, mental and spiritual health. This was followed by a question and answer session. As usual, for better or for worse, Max was an active participant and always the first to comment or ask a question.

"You know, Miss Meagan, I read an article in a recent issue of *Science News* that said that except for about two percent of diseases, genes aren't important at all in our susceptibility to disease. If I understood the article correctly, each of our 40-plus trillion cells is surrounded by a protein membrane and our genes are contained inside the cell within the nucleus in our chromosomes, in our DNA. What scientists now have discovered is that, say you have a gene that can cause a certain type of cancer; it can only cause cancer if it is activated by a trigger that is located on the cell membrane surface. These triggers are fired by things that happen in our environment, both physically and emotionally. So, what that means is that if you control your environment, you will never get cancer. Now isn't that cool!"

Miss Meagan responded with positive surprise. "Well thank you Max! That seems like a really good explanation for what we have been talking about this afternoon on epigenetics. It's nurture that's most important, not necessarily nature or your genetics."

I couldn't help my competitive, egocentric self, so I jumped in even though I knew Max was directionally correct. "Max, that's all nonsense! It's speculative and unproven. If you have the gene for multiple sclerosis or Huntington's disease, you are highly likely to get those diseases."

Max retaliated. "That's correct, but those two diseases fall in the two percent that I mentioned."

The debate raged on between us and it looked as if Max would prevail. Finally, Miss Meagan had to step in. "You both have good points, and we can continue our discussion and debate during tomorrow's lunch session. However, I suggest that neither of you take the other's argument as confrontational or personal."

Max couldn't control himself. "Miss Meagan, you must be kidding!"

"Alright that's all for this lunch discussion. Let's head back to class for our project on anthropology and human culture."

I made it back to the discussion table in Wisdom Room #1, much before Max. He was always the last to arrive. His ADHD just could not get him to focus completely on getting from point A to point B in a straight-line efficient manner.

As Max sauntered into class, sipping his green juice, one of his liabilities—clumsiness—switched on just as he was about to pass me seated at the table. He tripped on someone's inadvertently extended foot and poured the remainder of his green juice all over my dress and my papers on the table. I went ballistic!

"You're a clumsy idiot! You did that on purpose!"

"No I didn't. I'm sorry, Sandra. I just tripped."

"Yeah, right! I'll get you for this, you worthless moron!"

"Sandra! That's no way to speak to Max. I'm sure it was an accident. I suggest you apologize to him."

I was steaming, but I knew there was no way out at this point except to apologize, even if I didn't mean it at the time.

With a tone and high level of patronization, I gave in to Miss Meagan's request. "I'm sorry Max. I'm *sure* you didn't mean it."

Max stared at me. He knew I really didn't mean it.

"Alright class let's take a 10-minute break while I help Sandra clean up this mess."

What she didn't know was that the real mess was yet to happen.

The next day at school, I was still seething from the prior day's confrontation with Max. I knew it was wrong to hold a grudge, but at the time, I just couldn't help it. Sally and I entered class 10 minutes early and found him in the corner surrounded by several other boys. He was showing off in response to a dare from Ravi, a young Indian genius from Mumbai. Max had a metal nail and was rapidly inserting and removing it from the wall socket, enduring a brief electric shock from the standard 110 volts of alternating current. Fortunately, with rubber-soled canvas shoes he was not well grounded and did not get nearly the flow of amperage that would be dangerous, possibly deadly, with a solid grounding to earth. Still, the boys continued to egg him on.

"Bet you can't hold it in the socket for three seconds," dared Ravi.

Max responded and held it for three seconds, but didn't look too happy about it.

In the meantime, I moved to the water fountain and poured a glass of mineral water. I ambled over to the "Max Show" and watched with amusement as he considered his classmates' prompting for longer exposure to the electrical current—at that point he had gone four seconds.

So I decided to showcase myself and diminish Max's "electrical entertainment." I had enough understanding of the basic behavior of electricity to know that I could upstage him. I said, "Look that's not very difficult. I'll bet I can hold the nail for five seconds."

In unison, the boys all responded, "Woooow!"

With that I set down my glass of water and grabbed the nail from Max, knowing full well that my boots had more than two inches of compact dry leather insulation, much more effective than Max's thin canvas sneakers. I inserted the nail into the wall as Ravi clocked me on his watch to six seconds.

"Well, Max we have a new champion, six seconds. Hooray for Sandra!"

"Give me that nail Sandra! I'll show you! Alright guys, it's 10 seconds this time."

With that Max inserted the nail into the socket and tensely endured the electric shock he felt through his body. The boys were jumping fanatically and cheering him on.

"Maxie! Maxie! Maxie!

I picked up my glass of water, and accidentally stumbled over Ravi who was kneeling down watching Max's grimace as he passed the six seconds mark. In his excitement, Ravi had jerked his leg backwards, causing me to fall. As I fell my glass tipped out its contents and smothered Max's canvas shoes.

Sensing a clean and direct, full-voltage, full-current, short-circuit to ground, the circuit breaker shut off the current to the socket in a matter of seconds, but those seconds of a live charge left Max lying on the floor completely still and unconscious. The boys began screaming for help. I just stood there. It was just like the time when I accidentally pushed Sally down the stairs. I was simultaneously remorseful and scared, yet glad that Max got his comeuppance. The fact that both emotions filled my consciousness scared the daylights out of me. What was happening to me?

Fortunately, Miss Meagan had just entered the classroom.

"Oh my God, what's happened to Max?"

Ravi responded in a flash, "He stuck a nail in the wall socket and was fine until Sandra stumbled and spilled her water onto his sneakers. Then all hell broke loose. I think he's dead!"

Miss Meagan immediately ordered me to go to Wisdom Room #3 and bring back Mr. Shipley, who was a former medic in the U.S. Army. I left the room and Miss Meagan began to administer CPR as best she could. She had taken a course many years earlier, but never had to use it. The class was in complete disarray. Sally was standing next to Miss Meagan and knew by her telepathic connection to me that I had not yet gone to Mr. Shipley's room. Sally ran to his class as fast as she could and brought him back immediately. He knelt beside Max and administered an expert dose of CPR while Miss Meagan called 911.

By the time the rescue squad arrived six minutes later, Max was conscious and seemed to have recovered. They brought him to Ojai Valley Community Hospital for further observation. The good news was he was fine and able to go back to school that same day.

That afternoon Barry drove us home as usual. Sally and I were quiet for nearly the entire ride, and we both knew why. She broke the silence. "Why didn't you rush immediately to get Mr. Shipley to help Max?"

"I don't know Sally. I should have run as fast as I could, but something was holding me back. I can't explain it." I genuinely felt a deep remorse for what I had done, or more accurately, failed to do.

Sally looked at me and didn't say a word. She was only 10 years old, yet she understood well beyond that of most adults. She tried desperately not to show the tears welling up in her eyes, but I could see them in the reflection from her window. She continued to look away from me out the car window to the Pacific Ocean on our left as we drove home on U.S. Highway 101. We were so connected; I knew what she was thinking—*Oh my God, please help us.*

CHAPTER 6
DIFFERENT PATHS

"Do not go where the path may lead; go instead
where there is no path and leave a trail"
—Ralph Waldo Emerson

As Sally and I progressed through Wisdom Academy, it was clear to everyone who knew us that although we were exact physical mirror images of each other, inside, our souls were as different as night and day. Sally was seen as a compassionate team player, sensitive, always seeking the spiritual path, and as a consequence had a deep interest in the Eastern Wisdom Traditions.

I, on the other hand, was perceived as intense, retaliatory, fiercely competitive, and somewhat strange because of my keen interest in the black arts. These impressions were certainly well deserved. As a result, those who saw these differences were drawn to Sally but distant toward me. Many events that occurred over the years, starting with Max's near electrocution, supported these impressions. Most people looked at Sally as a lovable angel and at me as *The Bad Seed*, not unlike the character played by the then child actress Patty McCormick in the famous 1956 classic thriller film by the same name.

However, a significant potential benefit to both of us followed from Wisdom Academy's incredible success. As a consequence, Allison Bryan was able to expand the school's curriculum to support students until they were both socially and academically prepared to transition to a university. For most students this was generally at age 15 or 16. After testing, they usually entered the second or third year at their university of choice. Wisdom Academy had grown to nearly 80 students and was by then acknowledged as the world's premier school for highly gifted children.

At age 13, Sally and I were facing all of the social challenges that most teenage girls encounter in high school—dating, wild parties, competition within the student body for peer acknowledgment and support, and more. I must say that Sally handled this well by having open discussions with Mom and Allison, both of whom were very supportive.

In contrast, because of the conflicting emotional turmoil rummaging through me, I remained closed on most issues and projected a know-it-all attitude. Mom and Dad consistently intervened in my affairs and tried to be as supportive as possible. But I found it impossible to be responsive and forthcoming. The truth is I did not want any help, especially from Dr. Zang. To Mom's and Dad's dismay, I often and I must say, very unfairly, referred to him as, "That worthless Dr. Zang!"

At age 14, both Sally and I began training with Daman Hongren, a Chinese Zen master living in Ojai, known to his students as Master Dam. I was strictly interested in his courses in the martial arts. I quickly reached proficiency for a multi-degree black belt in Taekwondo and was considered the most able martial artist at the Ojai dojo.

Sally, on the other hand, progressed amazingly quickly to become an expert at meditation and pranayama breath control for elevating consciousness, as well as several of the martial arts. Because of her humility and incredible capabilities, Master Dam saw her as his informal young assistant. Those studying at his dojo, including older students, enjoyed Sally as a competent dedicated colleague. She was always available to help them and to complement Master Dam's stringent disciplinary approach to the martial arts and Eastern Wisdom philosophy.

That was not the case for me. I was a constant loner. I loved it; and I hated it. It was as if I was confronting the memory and imprint of some past wicked life, often resurfacing in what now could be a great life. This conflict, at times, was unbearable.

Although I excelled in martial arts at Master Dam's dojo, I chose not to study as intensely the Eastern Wisdom Philosophy courses he offered. Instead, I pursued a darker path. I was much most interested in black magic, ancient alchemy and any means to refine and extend my paranormal capabilities, even though this was strictly forbidden by Mom and Dad.

In the neighboring village of Meiners Oaks, I found a master of the black arts, an old Egyptian recluse named Master Bennu Tuat. Interestingly, *Tuat* in the ancient Egyptian language means "underworld." Master Ben, as he was known to most, was a late octogenarian, who had come to California from Luxor over 50 years ago. He settled in Ojai because of its spiritual energy and made a modest living as an astrologer, a tarot cards reader and part-time magician. Although an expert in many of the alchemical and Egyptian spiritual arts and mysticisms, Master Ben was cautious about touting their potential and careful not to use them among students and friends. For some reason, I was his only exception. He said he found what he called my "animal magnetism" much too alluring.

I was particularly attracted to him because he was an authority in hieroglyphics, the language of the original text of *The Egyptian Book of the Dead* written over 3,500 years ago. I desperately wanted to read the original text and learn the magic spells and other supernatural feats it disclosed. After much dedication and 18 months of study, I became quite adept in hieroglyphics and read the text several times, cover to cover. But the problems arose when I began in earnest to practice the spells described in the book.

Our family lived in a lovely old Andalusian style home inherited from Mom's parents. It was located in the Santa Barbara foothills on North La Cumbre Road just off Foothill Road. Although Mom and Dad had excellent jobs, they could never have afforded to buy this beautiful home in such a desirable neighborhood. Even the real estate taxes were a challenge for them. But it was a wonderful home for the entire family and especially for Sally and me; we both had our own bedroom and were thought by Mom and Dad to be well on our way to becoming physically and emotionally mature young ladies.

It was late on a Friday evening when Barry had driven Sally home from her martial arts class with Master Dam. She was sore and exhausted and was all set to take a hot bath and call it a night. As she entered the living room from the attached glass and stucco porch, she greeted Mom and Dad, both of whom were reading and sipping their favorite white wine, *Russiz Superiore Pinot Grigio.*

"Hi Mom; hi Dad! How was your day?"

"Great, sweetheart! Dad and I just came back from a yummy dinner in town at Ca' Darios. How about you? You look beat."

"I do feel a bit beaten up. I had several rounds this evening with Master Dam and he showed no mercy! It's just amazing what he can do at nearly 70 years of age!"

"Come over here sweetheart and give your Dad a big hug. I'll try to perk you up."

"I'm fine Dad. I just need a nice hot bath with some of Mom's magical essential oils and mineral salts and a goodnight's sleep. I'll be fine in the morning."

"Fine, you do that and sleep in tomorrow. It will be good for you."

"Dad, did you ask the chef at Ca' Dario for his recipe for that incredible sauce in his *Mussels Meunière*?"

"I did, for the fifth time; he said no way, it's apparently top secret!"

"Oh well…Is Sandra back from her hieroglyphics class with Master Ben?"

"She is. I think she's upstairs studying."

"Good night Mom, Dad."

"Good night sweetheart, sleep well," was Dad's response.

Mom added, "Your favorite crepes for breakfast tomorrow; just let me know when you and Sandra are up."

"Right, Mom."

Sally climbed the stairs to the second floor which housed three bedrooms, each with their own bathroom, and a separate room for Mom and Dad's joint office. Sally noticed that my door was closed and heard chanting coming from my room.

She walked to the door and put her ear closer to listen. Sure enough, she heard me chanting in a strange language, *maybe Egyptian,* she thought? She knocked but I did not respond. I was deep in meditation. She knocked again, and still, no response. Sally squeezed on the door handle and slowly opened the door. Then was shocked at what she saw.

The room was dimly lit. Only a small end table lamp next to the bed was on. And there I was, levitating three feet above my bed and chanting in what Sally correctly guessed to be an ancient Egyptian tongue.

Sally didn't know what to do. She was certainly aware that because of our exceptionally high levels of consciousness, we had powers way beyond normal. But we had sworn to our parents never to pursue them in any way. Our telepathic powers were a given. We could do little to "turn them off." But active pursuit of telekinesis, clairvoyance, remote viewing and other paranormal activity was completely off limits. Sally had never even thought about levitation. But I did.

She wanted to do something, yet she was afraid I might suddenly fall and hurt myself. At that very moment, I was telepathically aware of her concern. I stopped chanting and abruptly opened my eyes.

"Sister, why do you disturb me when I am in intimate conversation with Osiris?"

Sally didn't know what to say. She was well-read enough to know that Osiris was the Egyptian god of the dead or the underworld. Often pictured in ancient texts as a green-skinned man with a pharaoh's beard, mummy-wrapped legs and wearing a crown adorned with two large ostrich feathers at either side, holding his symbolic crook and flail, he was worshipped as Lord of the Dead until the suppression of Egyptian religion with the rise of Christianity in the Roman Empire.

I was very abrupt with Sally. "Speak, Sally! I will not falter."

"Sandra, what are you doing? Is this why you have been so immersed in your studies with Master Ben? We promised Mom and Dad we would never trouble them or others with our paranormal powers."

"Rubbish! I intend to develop my powers further and I don't want anyone to stop me. I am through being looked at as a freak of nature by our teachers, the kids at school and all of those doctors we have had to visit over the years. What I have learned from my studies with Master Ben can help me immensely—even though he foolishly advised against any experimentation."

"Sandra, you're frightening me."

With that I closed my eyes, chanted a brief incantation and slowly descended down to my bed. "Look, Sally, I have spent nearly two years learning hieroglyphics so that I could read the original text of *The Egyptian Book of the Dead* and several other ancient texts on what our modern culture considers as black art and magic. But I can tell you, with the super high level of consciousness that we were born with, we could develop and refine our powers beyond what anyone has seen for centuries in the modern world. In fact, most would consider it pure myth; but it's not. You just have to have the intense focus and know-how to direct your elevated consciousness, which is something we were both born with. This would enable us to assume very powerful positions in this troubled world. We could even force solutions to many of the global issues we are keenly aware of, solutions that most corporate and political types haven't the courage to pursue. We would become famous and highly recognized for our contributions. Don't you see?"

Sally was nearly in a hypnotic state of fear. "Sandra, you are really scaring me. This is crazy. We're only 15 years old, and yes, we were born with certain powers, but used incorrectly they could be most damaging to others and even to us."

"Dear sister, don't be such a frightened mouse. Don't you want to do something great in this world?"

"Yes, I do, but not that way."

"Dammit, Sally, sometimes you can be such a loser!"

And with that, I inadvertently projected a powerful dose of my telekinetic mental energy at the chair next to where Sally was standing. It slammed to the ground with a loud noise, smashing the top of Sally's foot. I didn't mean for that to happen. I just wanted to frighten her.

"Aaaaaaa, my foot," Sally screamed, as a sharp pain shot up her leg.

Dad ran to the base of the stairs. "Girls, is everything alright up there?"

I responded, "No problem, Dad. A chair just tipped over and slightly banged Sally's foot. But she's fine."

"Sally, are you okay?"

Sally took two deep breaths and then responded, "I'm fine, Dad. Not to worry."

But she wasn't fine. Her foot wasn't the problem. You could see from her expression that she saw a monster brewing in front of her.

Chapter 7
The Alchemist

"You can kid the world, but not your sister."
—Charlotte Gray

As paradoxical and unusual as it may seem for identical twins, Sally and I were rapidly growing farther and farther apart—that is until Roberto Paradiso entered our lives.

Roberto came to the Wisdom Academy from the prestigious *Talenta Acadamia* in Switzerland. His father was an Italian diplomat who was transferred to Los Angeles. At 15 years of age, Roberto was way beyond bright; he was athletic and had a private classical European education not unlike that provided to aristocratic children during the Renaissance.

Most obvious was his handsome appearance and charismatic personality. He could capture your attention with just a few comments and most interestingly, Roberto simultaneously projected authentic modesty as well as absolute self-assurance. He could move between suave and boyish humility as deftly as a Shakespearean actor.

Roberto made immediate friendships with both Sally and me, and although it was not initially obvious, he had a soft spot for Sally. For quite some time, my bloated ego blinded me to Roberto's affection for my sister. As far as I was concerned, this was the first and only boy to enter Wisdom Academy I felt was worthy of my time. I was particularly attracted to, and I must admit, entranced by his detailed picturesque stories of alchemy and witchcraft from the European Middle Ages. This was a subject that was near and dear to me.

Roberto wanted to become a neuroscientist. Ever since his father bought him a chemistry set for his tenth birthday, studying the history of alchemy was his hobby. He could quote the works of all the major European alchemists—Albertus Magnus, Roger Bacon, Paracelsus, George Ripley, John Dee, Robert Boyle, Fulcanelli, Nicolas Flamel and his most favorite of all, Sir Isaac Newton.

Roberto's interest in alchemy was based on his knowledge that true alchemy was not the way of medieval charlatans. Those quacks promised great wealth and unmitigated power to well-heeled aristocrats of their day, and all these wealthy nobles had to do was to heavily fund their efforts to turn lead into gold and create the long-sought-after *Elixir of Life.* Roberto noted that these tricksters promised they would eventually make the aristocrats wealthier and more powerful than their enemies and competitors. And on top of that, they would have the gift of immortality to enjoy their newly found assets. Presented properly, it was a deal that was difficult to refuse. The most persuasive reason was quite simple, *What if it really works and your enemies were to succeed before you?*

Roberto knew very well that authentic dedicated alchemists were men of great wisdom and elevated spiritual consciousness. In this male-dominated world, there were even several highly accomplished women alchemists, primarily prior to the chauvinistic Middle Ages, during the era of Arabic alchemy. Mary the Jewess, Kleopatra Chrisopoeia and Hypatia all appeared around the third century A.D. and made significant contributions that enabled European alchemy to thrive, and eventually give birth to the field of modern chemistry.

Roberto told Sally and me that European alchemists were modest and very cautious in their pursuits. They hid the results of their research efforts and their discoveries behind a convoluted mask of secret symbols and an arcane language for fear that this information might fall into the wrong hands. During the period of the Spanish Inquisition, they not only feared death by religious fanatics, but perhaps more devastating, their findings falling into the greedy hands of narcissistic, egomaniacal men.

To be perfectly frank, at the time, I was drawn to the potential witchcraft and black magic I thought to be associated with alchemy. But not Roberto. He saw a much higher vision in the work and dedication of the alchemists. In their experimentation, they not only sought to change ordinary materials into more highly developed substances, for instance lead into gold, but simultaneously through their link between spirituality and chemistry, to raise their own consciousness to much higher levels and thereby contribute to the evolution of the consciousness of the entire universe. In fact, this was above all their primary goal—not wealth and immortality. According to Roberto, authentic alchemists were not swindlers, con artists and quacks; they were the great oracles and seers of their day. And unknown to most of us today, Sir Isaac Newton was the premier "poster child" for European alchemy.

Roberto related with great fanfare and theatrics how Newton had done some of the most advanced research in alchemy, much more significant than what he had done in uncovering the universal laws of gravity, the calculus and classical mechanics. With some hesitation, he revealed to us that Newton secretly hid nearly all of his work in alchemy for fear that should it fall into the wrong hands it could be a disaster for humanity. This, of course, peeked Sally and my interest even more.

Roberto was excited to share with us the fact that most of the results of Newton's alchemy research had only recently been discovered in a locked, nondescript, wooden chest hidden in a dark corner of an attic at Trinity College, Cambridge University. He had begged and essentially coerced his father to use his British political contacts and clout to see that Roberto was introduced to the Cambridge Committee of Historical Science that was reviewing Newton's alchemical research.

Completely unaware of Roberto's superior intelligence, knowledge and immersion in alchemy history, they allowed him to read many of Newton's texts. As far as they knew, he was a young man who wanted to become a neuroscientist and was interested in the history of science. So why not enhance his scientific motivation? At least that was his father's argument to them. Roberto made extensive notes when left alone with the documents. He refused to tell us what he had learned. He said only that he was very concerned if there were even a shred of truth to several of Newton's findings.

One afternoon, while discussing the true nature of alchemy with Sally and me, to emphasize and justify his distress over what he had learned from the Newton chronicles, Roberto showed us a copy of a letter written by Newton to Sir Robert Boyle, one of the founding fathers of modern chemistry and an ardent 17th century alchemist. Boyle had written to Newton that he was close to uncovering the secret for transforming lead into gold.

Roberto cautioned Sally and me, "Look, I will let you read Newton's letter, which I managed to copy while at Cambridge studying his original texts. You mustn't mention it to anyone, or I will be in deep trouble with my father. But, before you read it, I need to give you a little background. Only then can you appreciate the importance and veracity of what Newton wrote to Boyle.

"In this letter, Newton is referring to the primary goal of the alchemist's research. It's called *Opus Magnum* or the "Great Work" and refers to synthesis of the Philosopher's Stone, sometimes called the *Mercurial Principle,* a minute amount of which was said to "catalyze" great wonders, most particularly, the transmutation of base metals such as lead into noble metals, such as gold. Properly prepared, it also had the potential to heal any illness and impart an extended lifespan, and in the best of cases, to induce immortality.

"Newton disclosed in one of his ledgers that while in France, he had several secret meetings with the famous alchemist, Nicolas Flamel. Now you may not find that so special until you are aware that Flamel was born in 1330, while Newton was born more than 300 years later in 1642!"

"But that's not possible!" asserted Sally.

Roberto delivered his response with much more than his usual theatrical flair and bravado. "It has been extensively disclosed in numerous alchemical texts that Flamel was one of the few European alchemists to have discovered the secret to synthesizing the Philosopher's Stone. He was allegedly immortal, both he and his wife! Why, he might be walking around here today, maybe here in Ojai!"

In his diary, Flamel said that he received much of the information for producing the Philosopher's Stone from a *converso*, a Jew who, under pressure from the Spanish Inquisitors had converted to Catholicism. He met this man while he was pursuing a personal spiritual journey in Spain walking the road to *Santiago de Compostela*. The converso was immediately drawn to Flamel's warmth, compassion and his genuine interest in making this a better world. He warned Flamel to be very careful with whom he shared his secret. In fact, it would be best if he told no one of its power."

Sally and I were in awe of Roberto's presentation.

"And now for the *pièce de résistance!*" exclaimed Roberto.

"You see, for all of his life, Flamel was a man of modest means. He worked as a bookbinder in Paris. But his heart was big, and even during his early economic station in life, he often helped the poor where he could. However, almost overnight, Flamel became an exceedingly wealthy man, one of the richest in France. And he gave much of his wealth away to build schools and hospitals in France. He helped the sick and the destitute. Now, where do think all of the wealth came from?"

Sally couldn't control herself, "Lead into gold!"

"Bingo!"

"Wow, I love it! Give me that letter!" I impatiently grabbed it from Roberto's hand and read it aloud.

Dear Sir Robert Boyle:

I urge you to keep high silence in addressing these alchemical principles because the way by which the Mercurial Principle may be impregnated has been thought fit to be concealed by others who have known it, and therefore may possibly be an inlet to something more noble that is not to be communicated without immense damage to the world if there be any verity in the warnings of Hermetic writers. There are other things besides the transmutation of metals which none but they understand.

Respectfully,
Isaac Newton

Sally was perplexed and concerned. "Roberto that sounds pretty serious. Do you suppose there is any truth to the subject of the correspondence between Boyle and Newton and his alleged meetings with Flamel?"

Roberto didn't respond, but looked intently at both of us.

"I mean, if there was a shred of truth to it, I don't think the pharmaceutical companies would be very happy. It would put them out of business. I guess my dad would have to look for a new job."

Roberto assured her, "You're right, Sally. But the bigger issue would be the ability for unsavory people to convert base metals like lead into gold. Gold would lose its value and the international financial markets would crash. It would be a global catastrophe!"

In my usual caustic manner at the time, I flippantly added, "This world could use a good shakeup!"

Roberto was not pleased with my comment, "Not like that, Sandra. You have no idea of the implications." He was getting agitated and you could clearly see he did not want to discuss the subject any further. "In any case, can we please change the subject? I have something exciting to share with you and Sally."

I wasn't about to let it go forever, but agreed with reservation, "Fine, Roberto; but I want to come back to this sometime soon."

"Great! So tomorrow afternoon I'm going to Ventura to begin lessons in rock climbing. Are you ladies interested? If so, you can join me. Mr. Shipley goes there a few days a week after classes and said he would drive me and bring me back to Ojai when I'm done. I'm sure he wouldn't mind if you both joined us."

Sally was excited to go. "How about it, Sandra? Let's do it! You're the super athlete in our family. What do you say?"

Reluctantly, I agreed, "Oh, alright, let's give it a shot."

Roberto expressed his enthusiasm for our participation. "Fantastic, I'm so glad you'll be joining me!"

Somehow, my ego thought his comment was meant especially for me. I couldn't be more mistaken.

Chapter 8
The Wall

"After climbing a great hill, one only finds
that there are many more hills to climb"
—Nelson Mandela

Our climbing instructor Miles Sanborn was not an easy guy to read. So, the three of us were quite impressed when he told us we were "beyond naturals" on the rock wall. He especially focused on me and asked if I had any prior experience. Wow, was that great for my thirsty ego! Climbing came easily to me, and I loved the absolute necessity to focus intensely on the moment, on the NOW. Present awareness was a critical part of my mystical training. In the real world of cliff climbing, focus was a mandatory skill and at times could mean the difference between life and death.

After six weeks of lessons, I could free-climb to the top of the wall at Vertical Heaven Climbing Gym in Ventura, easier and faster than either Sally or Roberto. Miles was amazed at my natural agility and asked me to enter a competition in Washington State, but I had no interest in pursuing it. I didn't want to leave Sally and, of course, Roberto.

The three of us liked the gym a lot. So, we were deeply disappointed when Miles told us they were closing up shop because the rent was raised to a level that could not support the business. Roberto suggested we take on some real cliffs and practice what we had learned at the gym. But first we decided to spend several weekends with Miles on modest size cliffs adjacent to Chief Peak in Ojai. It is one thing to climb an indoor rock wall, and it's another to manage the real thing.

At Chief Peak we climbed granite and sandstone cliffs and practiced hammering small metal spikes, called pitons, into the rock crevices as we climbed upward. Miles taught us how to safeguard our fellow climbers by *belaying* their climb from the base of the cliff. Typically, this is accomplished by fixing one end of a rope to the climber's harness using either of two popular safety knots, the *rewoven figure-eight* or the *bowline*. The rope is then passed through the eye of a piton which the climber has fixed into the rock wall as he climbs.

The long end of the rope falls earthward to a second person called the *belayer* stationed on the ground at the base of the cliff who also wears a harness with a belay device to which the rope is attached. This device enables the belayer to vary the amount of tension on the rope. In one position, the rope can run freely through the device; in the other, it can be held by the belayer without any movement of the rope. This is known as the "locked-off" position.

This is a very effective safety procedure, and prevents climbers from falling very far should their footing slip, or if one of the pitons works its way free from the cliff wall.

After several weeks of practice at Chief Peak and some planning, Roberto, Sally and I decided our first serious climb would be Sespe Gorge, located a 45-minute ride from Ojai in a scenic forest. There we found a challenging steep 120-foot granite cliff. The three of us had certainly challenged ourselves at the Vertical Heaven Climbing Gym, and we were among the best of the new climbers there. But the wall at the gym was only 30 feet at its highest point and the floor was a soft padded canvas. Even the modest 50-foot cliffs at Chief Peak were a relatively easy climb. Sespe Gorge would be the real thing, and there would be no trainer to guide us up the vertical stone wall.

Sally and I insisted on being treated equally with Roberto—no gentleman's concession where *the man goes first to stake out the risks.* By drawing straws, it was determined that Sally would climb first, belayed by Roberto. When Sally reached the top, she would return to our starting point by the meandering path behind the cliff. Then Roberto would climb, belayed by me, and subsequently Sally would belay me. This order meant that Sally got to place all of the initial pitons for the three of us.

After an hour or so discussing climbing strategy, Sally was set to go, sort of. As she put on her climbing harness and Roberto assumed his belay harness, it was apparent that she was frightened as she gazed up the cliff wall. Roberto tried to comfort and encourage her.

"Come on Sally, just do what you did at Chief Peak. You were brilliant! It doesn't matter whether the wall is 20 feet or 120 feet, the technique's the same, right?"

"Sure, but the falling distance is not, Roberto!"

"Look, you can do this. I have great faith in you and your abilities. The three of us have done amazingly well so far. Miles said we were his best students ever."

I didn't like where this conversation was going. In my biased egocentric mind, Roberto was being a bit too warm to Sally.

As he spoke increasingly softly to Sally, he moved closer towards her personal space. She was in a trance and it was clear she was losing her fear, or at least, unaware of it. Soon, he embraced her in his arms. I could not control myself. I was becoming more and more livid. Jealousy percolated through every cell in my body. I felt it deeply and didn't like it. My ego kept reiterating—*How could he do this to me? How could she do this to me? Sally was a traitor! It's pure and simple betrayal! How could she entice Roberto; and right here in front of me? Damn them both!*

Before Sally could do or say anything, Roberto kissed her gently on the forehead, then on each cheek and then, for just the slightest moment, on her lips. Neither of them said a word.

I disrupted the moment, exploding with negative energy. "Are you two serious about climbing or not? Let's get moving!"

Neither Sally nor Roberto said a word. She turned and faced the cliff and began to climb, with Roberto verbally supporting her with every step she took. I was beside myself. I wanted to spit, I was so angry. But, I had to control myself, and I did, by creating a number of retaliatory scenarios in my mind, things I could do that would attract Roberto to me. It was truly the thought process of the *Bad Seed*. I knew it and hated it, but I could not help myself, or maybe as I reflect back as honestly as I can, I didn't want to help myself. I was torn between an innate love for my sister, my passion for Roberto, and a jealousy streak beyond imagination. In retrospect, this was unrequited love at its best, if that's the right word.

One of the scenarios surfaced from my expertise in the black arts. *Would it work and win Roberto "back?" Maybe so.* At the time, my ego never for a moment allowed me to consider that Roberto had never been mine. With my mental scheme running through my mind, I was able to contain my anger for Sally and Roberto and what I thought at the time was their outright "betrayal."

Sally was much more agile than she had imagined. She slipped only once, and fell several feet when one of her pitons lost its grip in the rock crevice. Roberto had no problem halting her fall and encouraging her forward. But somehow, the fall didn't seem to bother her at all. As someone in tune to Sally's thoughts, I could see that her mental focus alternated between picking the right crevice for the next piton and Roberto's embrace and kisses before her climb. She had to work hard at pushing the latter thought from her reverie; she might make a wrong decision. Amazingly, she made it to the top in just under an hour. She and Roberto cheered her victory with great gusto and fanfare. I was noticeably silent. Sally knew why, and was not at all happy about hurting me. Roberto's feelings for her came as a total surprise; but she liked the way he touched her soul.

As Roberto and I waited for Sally to return, I edged in closer to him as he sat on a large rock smiling and enjoying Sally's success. In a moment of greater calm, I wanted to understand his true feelings for Sally.

"I couldn't help seeing your good luck caress and kisses for Sally. Is that your usual ceremony with female climbing friends?"

"I didn't plan that; it just happened."

"What about me; will it just happen as well?"

"Look Sandra, I really like both of you, but there's something special happening between Sally and me. I think she may sense it too. What do you think?"

I was quiet and contemplative for several seconds before responding. "I guess I thought that we had something special between us, Roberto."

"Sandra, I do like the both of you. You two are my very best friends—ever! It's just that…well…something's happening between Sally and me, something I never planned. You know what I mean?

"Yeah, right! Whatever."

At that moment, Sally came around the bend with a smile from ear to ear. "Wow! That was the most fantastic experience of my life!"

"You were super, Sally. I only hope that Sandra and I can do the same."

"You'll both be great, I just know it."

As usual, I broke the positive energy moment, "Well, we better get this show on the road if Roberto and I are going to make it to the top before dark."

And with that, Roberto put on his climbing harness and readied the ropes, while I suited up with the belay equipment. Facing the cliff wall at arm's-length distance, he leaned forward and put both palms flat on the wall. He went into a state of meditation to sharpen his sensory focus. He picked up the climbing rope at his feet and tied it securely to his harness. For the first time in his climbing experience, he decided to use a bowline knot. I'm not sure why—I don't think even Roberto knew why; especially, as Sally and I were always teasing him about the more complicated rewoven figure-eight knot. But his decision was about to come back to haunt me.

I quietly approached Roberto from behind, put my hands on his hips and whispered in his ear, "Are you ready pretty boy?"

"I'm all set and ready to go." With that he turned his head briefly to Sally, sitting on a rock several feet away to his left. Her hands were folded in apprehension and excitement, or perhaps in prayer.

He winked at her and said, "I'm off! Wish me luck!" I was noticeably disturbed, but didn't say a word.

Roberto scampered up the first 10 feet with the grace of a ballet dancer. He located the first piton set by Sally and threaded the belay rope through the eye of the piton and attached it to his harness. *This was going to be a piece of cake!*

As he ascended the cliff face, Sally offered words of support; I was as quiet as a mouse. Regretfully, I was scheming; getting prepared to carry out my plan. Roberto's last comments to Sally sealed my decision.

Neither Sally nor I had anything to say to each other as Roberto scaled the cliff. Sally was giving all of her attention to Roberto. My communication was only with him and it was strictly in response to his requests for more rope or a tighter rope, as the case might be.

Halfway up the cliff at about the 60-foot mark, Roberto stopped to take a few minutes rest as he clung to the precipice wall. His ascent to that point had been flawless.

Now is the time, I thought.

CHAPTER 9
RETRIBUTION

"Stronger than lover's love is lover's hate.
Incurable, in each, the wounds they make."
—Euripides, from his play, *Medea*

I had learned much more than meditation with Master Ben. He was one of the few masters in this part of the Western world who was an expert at guiding consciousness-gifted students to perfect the paranormal skills they were born with. Through his efforts, and unknown to anyone, I had become proficient at levitation, telepathy, telekinesis and remote viewing. It was the latter two skills I would exercise that afternoon. Master Ben had cautioned me that flagrant and careless display of these skills could be very dangerous. I promised to follow his instructions and adhere to his warnings. For the most part, I had kept my promise. However, there was one occasion on which I used my remote viewing skills in a somewhat cavalier, though fortunately, harmless manner.

My classmates and I at Wisdom Academy were taking our final exam in philosophy. Question number 11 asked, "Who was the author of *The Fourth Way*," a book that explains in great detail the philosophy of the Greek-Armenian philosopher, G. I. Gurdjieff. Having finished the test well before the entire class, and feeling quite bored, I began to use my remote viewing skills to read the test papers of the other students. I had no interest in cheating. I was too smart and too sure of myself for that. I was simply killing time and relieving my boredom.

When I came to Roberto's paper, I noticed that all of his answers were, certainly in my view, correct except for question 11. When class was dismissed, I teased Roberto and told him that all of his answers were correct except for number 11. *It was totally wrong!*

"No it's not!" was his retaliation. "And how would you know anyway, I sit in the front of the room and you're in the very last seat. The answer is simple, *The Fourth Way* was written by Gurdjieff."

"No it wasn't!" was my triumphant return. "It was indeed a series of Gurdjieff's lectures which were compiled by his star student, P. D. Ouspensky, but they were published posthumously by Ouspensky's students."

Sally offered her condolences, "So sorry, Roberto, but Sandra is correct."

"Okay, maybe so; but how in the world did you know I had the incorrect answer?"

"It was just a lucky guess on my part," was my response, with just a glimmer of a pompous smile.

Roberto was mystified. How could I just guess his incorrect answer? And, in the end, he saw that I was correct; it was the only question he missed out of 30 on the test? He mentally filed this experience as a red flag; *there is something not right with Sandra. Caution!*

That afternoon at Sespe Gorge would be Roberto's second experience with my *paranormal skills.* As Sally sat nearby on top of a four-foot boulder cheering on Roberto while he rested at the 60-foot mark, I went into an instantaneous deep meditative trance. I mentally followed Roberto's rope in my mind's eye up to his harness and clearly viewed the bowline knot he had tied to the clip on his harness. *A bowline, that's strange. What happened to his favorite rewoven figure-eight?* I proceeded with my plan. Calling on my telekinesis skills, I quickly detached the knot, simultaneously pulling on the rope so that it fell towards the ground through five of the safety pitons.

Roberto saw it happen and was shocked beyond disbelief.

"Oh my God, Sandra! I've lost my rope! But how could that be? It was tied securely!"

Sally screamed in desperation and called out to Roberto, "Hold on! Don't move! Sandra and I will bring the rope to the top of the cliff and we will lower it to you. You can tie up and the two of us can lower you safely to the ground."

"Sally, I can't hold on that long. My fingers are already cramping. I'm afraid I am going to fall!"

As I had carefully planned, I took charge. "Roberto, please hold on, just for a short time. I will help you."

"Sally, hold on to this belay rope and attach it to your harness!"

Before Sally could utter a word, I was scaling the cliff freestyle as if I were a seasoned mountaineer.

Almost in unison, Roberto and Sally screamed as loud as they could, "Sandra, no!" But I gave a deaf ear to their pleas.

In record time, I had grabbed the loose end of the rope as it sat some 15 feet below Roberto, and rapidly climbed immediately below his tiring body. "Roberto, don't move an inch!" He was paralyzed and could say nothing. His fingers and hands were in immense pain frozen into the side of cliff, holding perilously to a two-inch overhang and his toes were in the same shape wedged in a slightly larger outcropping.

"Next time, Roberto, use a *double* bowline and not a single."

Although nearly in a state of shock, my comment registered concern in Roberto's mind, but he said nothing. He couldn't. He was frozen to the cliff side.

With that, I moved up alongside and slightly below him, my arms parallel to his waist. I managed to find a larger outcropping for support so that I could use one of my hands to reconnect his harness rope. Neither of us said a word as I struggled to tie a double bowline knot to his harness. "Now listen carefully, Roberto. You're in no shape to conquer this cliff today. You're now secured and Sally can belay you safely to the ground."

In barely a whisper he said, "But what about you?"

"Don't worry about me; I will be safely on the ground well before you."

"No, Sandra, please no!"

But before Roberto could comment further, I was making my way down the cliff side with the same dexterity I had used to reach Roberto. *This courageous act would surely win him over!* My egocentric jealousy blinded my intelligence beyond my personal recognition. I never for one moment realized that I had put Roberto in death's way just to carry out my foolish plan.

When I reached the ground, Sally was crying profusely. "Sandra, are you crazy? You could have been killed!"

Without saying a word, I grabbed the belay rope from Sally, attached it to my harness and talked Roberto down to the bottom.

When he reached the ground, the three of us hugged in unison for a good five minutes or more. No one said a word. Roberto was physically and emotionally drawn. Sally was still overwhelmed in tears. But me, I was as calm and stoic as if I had just returned from the grocery store.

After our fears had settled to a manageable level, my world came tumbling down on me. Roberto came forward with the two concerns that bothered him when I approached him from below on the wall.

"I can't for the life of me understand how my knot could have possibly come undone. A bowline is one of the safest knots known."

Sally looked surprised. "Roberto you never use a bowline; your favorite knot has always been the rewoven figure-eight! Could you possibly have tied it incorrectly?"

"Impossible, Sally. We practiced these knots with Miles until we could do them in the dark. Roberto turned and looked at me with a serious expression that I had never seen on him before. "Sandra, how did you know I had tied a single bowline knot to my harness?

All of these weeks that we have been climbing together, as you well know, I never once used a bowline; it's always been the rewoven figure-eight.

"You and Sally consistently teased me for using a more complex knot than required. Only for this climb did I decide to use the bowline just like you and Sally. I tied it to my harness as I faced the cliff wall just before climbing. You could not possibly have seen the knot at that point. When you free-climbed to a position just below me on the wall, there is no way you could have seen it then either. If anything, based on past experience you would have assumed I used the rewoven figure-eight."

I just stared at Roberto and Sally. She didn't say a word.

"Look, I'm very appreciative of what you did. You risked your life to save mine and for that I will be forever in your debt."

"Oh, Roberto, it was just a lucky guess."

Roberto was dumbstruck.

"You mean a lucky guess like the time you guessed I had answered question 11 incorrectly on our philosophy final exam?"

I didn't say a word, nor did Sally. But I could see within her mind; she was deeply concerned, but didn't dare raise her thoughts. She knew what had happened and didn't like it at all. She experienced the same fear when she caught me levitating in the bedroom.

This was a terrible turning point for the three of us, and had things stayed the way they were when we returned from Sespe Gorge, my relationship with Roberto and Sally would have deteriorated beyond repair and not only destroyed any semblance of caring among the three of us, but also ravaged the close-knit fabric of my family.

But I would have an epiphany and it would change the remainder of my short life on earth and in fact, my life forever.

CHAPTER 10
RESOLUTION

*"How few there are who have courage enough to own
their faults or resolution enough to mend them."*
—Benjamin Franklin

Although Sally and Roberto could never forget what happened at Sespe Gorge, they tried their best to bury their concerns. They both clearly understood my feelings for Roberto and my jealousy of Sally, and they were sensitive to not put us in situations that would make things worse.

As for me, I finally woke up and realized the terrible events I had caused at Sespe Gorge. However, I still had significant obstacles to overcome.

The rest of the year at Wisdom Academy was challenging for the three of us, not academically, but socially; perhaps even spiritually. Even though they were sensitive to me, it was clear that Sally and Roberto were growing closer and closer together. They did not actually date, but their free time was nearly always together. And when there was any semblance of a date, it was the three of us together. This was terribly frustrating for me. It was a time of jealousy and resentment; a time of mistrust and thoughts of retribution—even though Roberto and Sally were meticulously careful to avoid any signs of their feelings in my presence.

For the first time, as these negative emotions surfaced time and again, I became aware of the demon I was fighting and I wanted to set things right, but did not quite know how. The three of us were abundantly aware of the constant tension among us. It was difficult for me to control my thoughts about using my sorcery powers. Deep down, very deep, I really didn't want to cause any harm to either Sally or Roberto. I loved them both. But I was caught between this rock and a hard place and I desperately wanted to crawl out.

As time moved on through the year, I increasingly felt the sanctity of my sorority and love for Sally. I had an awakening as a result of the incident at Sespe Gorge. I was trying hard to accept the reality of Roberto and Sally's relationship and to control the superpowers I had developed by combining my advanced innate skills with my training under Masters Dam and Ben.

But there were few places to hide from my feelings. Somehow, I had to deal with the issue and find peace in my challenged world; a world of disappointment, jealousy, regret and anguish. I had to find some hope for a better future. And at that point in time I seemed to be on my own, which I finally realized was all of my own doing.

I resorted to spending more and more time at Master Dam's dojo, mostly in martial arts, sparring with the best of the black belt opponents who came from all over to study with him. It was a good energetic outlet for my negative emotions. I had mastered a number of paranormal skills with Master Ben, and sought no more training in that area. I had demonstrated this adeptness when the three of us were climbing the wall at Sespe Gorge. But I was now genuinely careful not to call on these powers. I even worked hard at disconnecting from telepathy with Sally, especially when Roberto was around.

My athletic prowess in the martial arts went too far one evening when sparring with a young Korean man. Twenty-two-year-old Joon Rae Kim had an advanced black belt in Taekwondo and had just moved to Ojai from Seoul. He ran a small dojo there and was a distant cousin to Master Dam. Master Dam, who was approaching

70, convinced Joon to move to Ojai and begin the process of taking over his business.

On this particular evening, Roberto, Sally and I had gone to an early movie at the Ojai Playhouse to see the popular film *Love Actually*, starring Hugh Grant, Martine McCutheon and Liam Neeson. Sally was an avid Hugh Grant fan and had read great reviews of the film. It followed eight very different couples dealing with their love lives in various loosely interrelated tales, all set during a frantic month in London just before Christmas.

Leaving the theater, Sally and Roberto were enthralled with many of the scenes and were bursting with conversation about the film. I was my normal quiet self under these circumstances of high interaction between Sally and Roberto.

Roberto asked enthusiastically, "What about you, Sandra, what did you think of the movie?"

"Oh, it was okay. I thought it was trying too hard to show a meaningful message through the connections among the couples and their love lives."

Sally chimed in, "Oh Sis, I thought it did a great job at that. And besides, it was only a film. Don't take it so seriously. It was a great escape from our normal hectic week at the academy."

"I guess you guys are quite the experts on love lives, right?"

"Come on Sandra! I tell you what; what do say, you, Sally and I go across to the arcade and get an ice cream? My treat, okay?"

"No, I don't think so. I have my gym clothes in my backpack. I'm going to the dojo for a workout. There's a new black belt who just came from Korea and I would like to spar with him." I was really saying, *I'm tired of you two tonight. I've got to work off some of this steam.* "So Sally, when Barry comes by later to pick us up at Libbey Park, please drive by the dojo on Matilija to pick me up."

"Will do. Enjoy, Sis!"

With that, I grabbed my backpack and walked three blocks to the dojo on West Matilija Street. When I entered, I was greeted by Master Dam.

"Sandra, I have someone I want you to meet."

"This is Joon Rae Kim, my cousin from Korea. He will be gradually taking over the dojo. I will still be here for the classes on Eastern Wisdom and Philosophy, but he will take over teaching martial arts."

"Joon, this is Sandra, perhaps the most gifted student I have had in my 50 years of teaching martial arts."

"Wow Sandra! That is quite an endorsement coming from Master Dam!"

"Thank you. Do I call you Joon?"

"Sure that's fine. Would you like to work out this evening with Taekwondo?"

"Sure. I will change and be back in a few minutes."

When I left to change, Joon, highly trained in Eastern Wisdom and Philosophy, looked a bit perplexed at Master Dam. He offered, "There is something troubling this young lady."

"You are right. Recently, she has been coming here much more frequently, just for workouts in martial arts. I can see by her moves that she is fighting a demon. Be careful with her; anger flows through her body and she does not yet recognize the potential of her power."

"Thank you, Dam."

When Joon and I walked on to the mat, before initiating combat, we offered each other the traditional bow and greeting. But Joon could see that I was filled with a level of anxiety. It was also clear after just two minutes of combat that I was one of the most gifted opponents he had ever faced.

A few minutes later, Joon saw me assume the *Dwi-gibi Sogui* stance which is used in preparation to perform a powerful kick attack. He was prepared for my attack, but he was not prepared for the full force I applied, something no martial artist ever does in sparing matches. Joon correctly blocked my kick with his right arm, but the force I used sent him reeling in pain to the mat.

"Oh my God, Joon. I'm so sorry," as I knelt beside him.

Master Dam came running to the two of us on the mat. "Sandra, what did you do?"

"Master Dam, I'm so sorry. I made a terrible mistake."

"You certainly did. Please go sit down while I attend to Joon."

I sheepishly sauntered to the sideline benches.

"Joon are you okay?"

"I'm fine Dam. With some hot and cold compresses, it will be fine in the morning. Dam, I have an idea. Please allow me to speak privately with Sandra. I am closer to her in age; maybe I can help her."

Master Dam thought for several seconds. "Okay, I trust your intuition."

Joon walked to the bench and sat beside me. I was nearly in tears.

"I'm so sorry, Joon. This last year has been difficult for me. I seem to be angry at everyone, and it shows in what I do. I never intended the force behind that kick. It just happened. Up until last year, I could care less about my negative feelings. But something happened to me along the way and I have begun to see clearly the anguish I cause my parents, my sister and my friends."

"Sandra, may I share a thought with you?"

"Of course."

"You know, to love someone, you must first love yourself. To be angry with someone, you must first be angry with yourself. And when I say 'yourself,' I mean your *Self*, your soul, the very core of your being. *To show love, you must first know love, and to show anger you must first know anger. Knowing always starts with your Self.*"

I looked at Joon in a bewildered state. I was devastated and could say nothing. I wasn't just the revengeful young lady who for the last 15 years had plagued my family and especially my twin sister, Sally, with stress, strain and acts of emotional torture.

"You are very talented in the martial arts, and I would like to get to know you. Before you leave for home, will you join me at the *Plaza Pantry* for a cup of tea?"

I wasn't sure this was a good idea, but I agreed to go, and I am so glad I did.

"Master Dam, when Bruce and Sally arrive, will you please ask them to pick me up at the *Plaza Pantry*?"

"Will do." He was hoping that this unfortunate evening would precipitate a friendship between Joon and me that would guide me in the right direction.

But I still had a long way to go. Master Dam knew it, but more importantly, I knew it.

CHAPTER 11
THE CATALYST

"Love is the most powerful catalyst. It can
change a heart and the world."
—Debasish Mridha

A challenging chapter was about to open in the lives of Roberto, Sally and me, and in fact, for the entire Brunel family. It started one Friday afternoon. Sally had been sniffling, coughing and wheezing for several days, but late that afternoon at school, she had the onset of a fever. Barry went to the Wisdom Academy to pick her up and brought her home. She didn't even undress, but buried herself under the covers and fell fast asleep. The reception office at the academy had notified Mom and she arrived home shortly after Sally had gone to bed.

She found Sally fatigued and shivering almost beyond control. A 400 milligram dose of ibuprofen helped to reduce the fever and shivers, but this didn't seem like a normal flu. By 2:00 am Saturday morning, it was clear that Sally was very ill. She was burning up with a 104-degree fever and had frequent coughs from deep within her lungs. Her ribcage ached with pain from violent bouts of uncontrollable heaving.

Dad immediately called Dr. Prescott, our family physician. At 74, Dr. Prescott, a Santa Barbara native, was an "old-school" physician, so he immediately came to our home to check in on Sally. After 10 minutes with her, he went down to the living room and spoke with Mom and Dad.

"I don't like what I hear in Sally's lungs. I'm not a pulmonary specialist, but from my experience, I'd say Sally has a serious case of walking pneumonia, more properly known as *viral pneumonia*. Usually, it can be treated with extended bed rest at home, but I feel that for some reason the alveoli in her lungs are quite full with fluid.

"What are alveoli?" Mom asked.

"They're little sacs on the surface of the lungs that excrete carbon dioxide and absorb oxygen. She's having difficulty breathing and may need oxygen to help her fight this off."

Dad immediately jumped in, "So what should we do; bring her to the hospital in the morning?"

"I wouldn't wait that long. I'd get her over to Cottage Hospital as soon as possible. From here it's a 10 minute ride by car; no sense calling an ambulance."

Mom grabbed Dr. Prescott's arm, "Dear God, doctor; is it that serious?"

"Look Margaret, to be frank, I'm not sure. There is little I can do out of my travel case. She needs quick access to blood tests and other diagnostic tools. I can call over to the hospital and help with an immediate admission and diagnosis."

Dad, though still in his pajamas and slippers, already had his coat on and was climbing the stairs to help Sally into the car. "Margaret, put some of Sally's things in a suitcase while I help her out of bed and into the car." Teary-eyed Mom hustled as quickly as she could, and Dad and Sally were off to Cottage Hospital. She followed several minutes later after dressing.

The next eight hours were trying for our family. After a complete blood panel, a computer tomography scan and a sputum culture, it was clear that Sally definitely had a serious case of viral pneumonia. It was so advanced that in addition to being put on concentrated oxygen, the medical staff in the pulmonary unit prescribed a bronchoscopy which would allow them to observe the *alveoli* air ways and see how challenged Sally's lungs actually were. It's quite an uncomfortable procedure, especially with patients who are barely cognizant of what's happening. It involves carefully snaking a long one-quarter inch diameter flexible rubber tube with a micro TV camera on its end through the trachea and into the lungs.

Things were not looking good for Sally. She was only occasionally conscious and when she was, she only wanted water to quench her thirst from dehydration and kept asking, "Where are Sandra and Roberto?"

Early that morning, Barry had driven me to the Wisdom Academy to pick up Roberto. We arrived at the hospital at about 8:00 am. Since viral pneumonia is not highly contagious, the staff allowed us both into Sally's room. She was now in the intensive care unit (ICU), hooked up to several monitors that follow critical bodily functions. Mom and Dad were sitting across the room sipping on black coffee from the hospital cafeteria.

"Hi Mom, Dad."

Dad was in deep thought, but Mom managed to respond.

"Hi honey. Hi Roberto."

"Hi Mr. and Mrs. Brunel. How's she doing?"

"About the same."

Roberto walked slowly to one side of the bed and I to the other. Almost on cue, we simultaneously reached for one of Sally's hands. She was not conscious.

"How are you doing Sis? I brought a funny looking Italian with me."

"She's really out of it. I guess she can't hear us, Sandra."

A second later, Sally opened her eyes and smiled first at me and then at Roberto. She immediately drifted off again. She seemed to be pleased to see both of us, perhaps because we seemed to be in a mutually cooperative and supportive mood, something she hadn't seen very often in the past.

Finally awakened from his contemplation, Dad added, "She'll be fine. She just needs lots of rest, fluids, and most of all, TLC from the four of us."

"Alan, I hope you're right. I don't like the way she looks. And there she is on oxygen and several monitors in the ICU. We need to stay close to the doctors."

"I agree, honey. But worrying is not going to help."

"Dad's right, Mom. We need to send positive energy towards her. From everything I have learned over the years from Masters Dam and Ben, I know it's the most powerful medicine. It can activate the body's internal pharmacopeia. That's the magic behind so-called "miracle healing," and on top of that there are no side effects."

"I guess you're both right. Why don't we take turns staying with Sally?"

Roberto offered, "I'll be happy to take the first shift while you folks go home and get some rest."

"Thanks, Roberto. Alan and I will be back later this afternoon. Then Barry can drive you back to Ojai. I will ask the nurse at the ICU reception desk to call us if there are any important changes."

"Fine, Mrs. Brunel. I'll be here."

I thought about staying with Roberto, but felt that would be awkward with Sally not awake. I decided to go home too and get some sleep, then take the night shift with Sally. I was beginning to feel a change in my soul—and I liked it.

Barry picked up Roberto at 3:30 pm and drove him back to his school dorm in Ojai as Mom and Dad settled in at the hospital until I arrived at 8:00 pm to relieve them.

"Hi Mom, Dad. How's she doing?"

"Not much change, honey. They continue to feed and hydrate her intravenously, and Roberto said she did wake up for about five minutes this afternoon, but wasn't very conversant. She just asked for you, Sandra. Did you have dinner, yet?"

I felt a growing presence of Sally's love. A couple of beats passed before I responded to Mom's question.

"A bit, I wasn't very hungry. Why don't you both go home and get something to eat and a good night's rest? I slept all afternoon, so I'm ready to stay until morning."

"Alright, that sounds fine. But be sure to have them call if there is any meaningful change in Sally's condition."

"Will do, Dad."

With that, Mom and Dad both kissed Sally on the forehead and then me, and left for home.

I sat quietly in a chair next to Sally's bed and tried to read Dostoyevsky's *The Idiot*, but it was too heavy for the current situation; I had a challenging time focusing, which was not normal for me. All I could think about was my life growing up with Sally, something I never gave one iota of thought to before then.

I recalled that no matter how many times I let Sally down, she always stood up for me to our parents, to our schoolmates, and even to Roberto. I remembered the incident when we were at the Wisdom Academy and I nearly killed Max by electrocution. I didn't intend to, but that was nearly the end result. Because of our telepathic skill, I was aware that Sally knew exactly what had happened; how I stalled getting help to save Max. Fortunately, because of Sally's telepathic capability, she was aware of what I was doing and raced off to Mr. Shipley's class to save the day—more critically to save Max! In retrospect, I am forever grateful.

Why have I been so tough on Sally, and why has she always been so loving and forgiving? The bigger question is why have I always been so jealous of her, and so angry? Why am I angry, and who is the real target of my anger? Joon would say it's me! Maybe I'm angry at myself for the terrible feelings I often have and for the times I've acted on them.

At that very moment, Sally began to stir. She rolled on her side facing me and opened her eyes. It was only for a few seconds, but she managed a smile.

"Hi Sis, how are you feeling?" But Sally had no strength to respond. She closed her eyes and was off again to the quiet of a semi-comatose state.

I continued my rumination about our childhood together. I was very clear about one thing—although I envied Sally's spiritually-adept personality, which was clearly very different than my predisposition, I knew without a doubt I would be lost without her. I had to find a way to change myself; I was the problem, not Sally. But how? Perhaps, Master Dam, Master Ben or possibly Joon could help me.

My reverie was instantaneously interrupted by a beeping on one of Sally's monitors. Two doctors rushed into the room.

"What's wrong doctor?

"Her fever is going off the chart! Somehow she seems to have gone into a state of sepsis. But it just doesn't make any sense."

"You mean blood poisoning?"

"Yes."

"But how could that happen?

"I don't know at this point; but I'm going to find out. But first, we must immediately put her on an ice bed to bring down her fever; it's 107 and rising! Please call your parents and ask them to come to the hospital immediately."

I relayed the message to the receptionist and when I returned, the doctors had already left the room having put her on an ice bed which was mechanically refrigerated to the freezing point of water. Her temperature had returned to normal, but Sally was still not moving.

"I have to do something for you Sally. I can't just let you lay there and die. I only pray that it will work. It is the cosmic force field I learned to access for levitation. I found the technique among the spells in *The Egyptian Book of the Dead*. I practiced and practiced, and finally learned how to focus all of my meditative energy simultaneously into all 40-plus trillion cells in my body. By doing so, I can control their collective functions, including their reaction to gravity. We're going to detoxify your cells, and bring you back to some level of normality."

With that, I assumed a lotus position on the chair in which I was sitting. I instantly assumed a deep meditation, going deeper and then deeper. I had become quite adept at doing this. I focused all of my energy on Sally. Her body began to tremble. It rose about three inches off the ice bed. I intensified the process. Then she began to make strange sounds. The needles on all of the monitors began to rise and fluctuate just below the setting that would activate the alarms. Then in just a few seconds of time, the needles on all of the monitors screamed to the maximum setting activating all of the alarms. Sally's body descended the three inches and she lay there in the ice bed, the alarms blasting away. I was in a totally exhausted state, and nearly unconscious. My focused meditation and spell casting sucked out nearly all of my physical energy.

The doctors raced into the room, but, by that time all of the alarms were off and the monitors had returned to normal.

"What in the world is happening here?" was the question to me by the first doctor to enter the room. I could hear them but I did not reply, still in a semi-conscious state.

A moment later, Sally was screaming, "I'm freezing! Why is this bed so cold?" She sat up and appeared drowsy, but nearly normal. A few seconds later, Mom and Dad ran into the room.

Sally welcomed them with a smile, "Mom, Dad!"

Dad responded, "Honey, are you okay?"

"I sure am. Please get me off this slab of ice!"

The doctor was all over Sally with an optical thermometer in her ear, looking in her throat, listening to her lungs and feeling her pulse. All appeared normal.

"I don't understand. Minutes ago she was burning with a dangerously high fever and now her temperature is 98.6! There is absolutely no inflammation in her throat, and I can't hear a thing out of the ordinary in her lungs! That's just not possible! Where in the world did all of the sepsis in her body go?"

Now a bit more recovered, I quietly speculated, "Maybe her blood stream somehow detoxified."

"I don't see how that's possible, but we'll see when we check her urine. In fact, Sally, you'll need to stay with us until tomorrow morning. We will need to do several tests to be sure you're completely recovered."

"Well, doctor, I don't know what's possible or not possible, but what I'm seeing in that bed, I'll take," was Dad's response.

Mom was smiling brightly as well, but she had something rolling around in the back of her mind.

"Sandra, you look terrible. Are you okay?"

"I'm fine, Mom; just a bit tired from last night's watch."

"Were you the only one in the room with Sally?"

"Yes, Mom."

"And, did you notice anything unusual?"

"Not really."

"I see … well in any case, let's not look a gift horse in the mouth!"

Mom knew Sally and me very well, better than we were ever aware of. She had a thought. *But perhaps, it was better left unsaid.*

Mom, Dad and I lingered for a time as Sally rested. While pleased with Sally's recovery, they were as perplexed as the doctors, by what appeared to be more than a minor miracle.

The next morning, Dr. Pearce entered Sally's room at 7:30.

"Sally, the specialists here are baffled. All tests indicate you are completely healthy. Your urine contained the highest concentration of dead toxic microbes the doctors here have ever seen. It was so concentrated it nearly looked like maple syrup! It was as if all of the toxins in every one of your cells entered your blood stream and were destroyed and then filtered out by your lone kidney. How they met their end, no one can fathom."

"Fantastic, Doc! Can I leave?"

"Yes, your mom will pick you up at 10:00 o'clock this morning. All the release papers should be completed by then."

"You know, Sally, there's another aspect to what happened to you that defies all medical knowledge and logic. Somehow, you were instantly stricken with intense sepsis by a bacteria known as *E. corrodens;* it's not the most common source of sepsis. But what is stranger yet, perhaps even troubling, is the fact that *E. corrodens* was exactly the same bacterial agent that caused your sepsis when you were born and ultimately led to you losing your right kidney."

"Now, that's spooky Doc. It's almost as if the Universe used *E. corrodens* to bring about certain changes throughout my life."

"That's as far out an explanation as any I've heard yet."

"Doc, you never know!"

Changing the subject to a more rational and logical focus, Dr. Pearce enquired, "Sally, do you have any recollection as to what might have happened to you to bring about this seemingly miraculous recovery?"

"Not really, Doctor Pearce. One moment I was staring into Sandra's eyes; I saw that she was crying, then I faded out. A brief time later, I felt a powerful energy force running through my body, and the next thing I knew I was freezing my butt off on that ice bed."

"I see, I see. Well, I guess we may never know what transpired here yesterday. All that matters now is that you have recovered. And for that, we are all very grateful."

"I can't wait to get out of here to be with Mom, Dad, Sandra and Roberto. I want to especially thank Sandra!"

"Thank her for what?"

"Well, ah, ah, I guess for being with me when I was down and out and needed her."

Again, Dr. Pearce's response was, "I see, I see."

But this time in his tone of voice, Sally could detect a subtle distinction. *Something doesn't feel right here. You're not being completely open with me, Sally.*

CHAPTER 12
THE CHOICE

*"In any moment of decision, the best thing you can
do is the right thing, the next best thing is the wrong
thing, and the worst thing you can do is nothing."*
—Theodore Roosevelt

Things seemed to be going in the right direction for Sally, Roberto and me. I was finally beginning to accept the fact that Sally and Roberto were closer than friends and that I and Roberto were simply very good friends. Most of the time that was fine with me. I had come a long way since Sally's episode in the hospital.

More than once, Sally felt grateful for the way the intermingled lives of our "trio" were going. She wondered how I had made such a big change, and thought back to Max's comments on epigenetics. Maybe nurture can have a much greater impact than nature. She liked to think that Roberto's entrée into our lives made all the difference in the world, and just maybe, was responsible for some of my changes.

In a way she was right. My near-electrocution of Max was certainly a wakeup call, but it was my jealous stupidity in putting Roberto's life in jeopardy on the cliffs at Sespe Gorge that really began the process of helping my soul cross into a space that would have some sense of normalcy and the love I always had deep down for Sally, Roberto and my family.

In any case, it really didn't matter. What did matter was that the three of us were on a more exciting and fulfilling course in our lives together.

Sure, I did have occasional moments tinged with a level of negative energy, but my new friendship with Joon filled a much-needed vacuum and he provided spiritual guidance to help me navigate through my occasional bouts of jealousy and resentment. He often reminded me that the Cosmos "knows" all, and always creates change that is optimal for the continued evolution of Cosmic Consciousness. Mom and Dad also felt the changes and could see a bright future for all those we were close to. However, that future was about to take a most unfortunate turn.

Roberto's 16th birthday party was planned to be a very special event. His parents, living in the Brentwood section of Los Angeles wanted to make it a most memorable occasion for him. They booked the beautiful Anacapa Ballroom at the Ojai Valley Inn & Spa. Mario and Isabella Paradiso invited more than 250 friends from all over the world. These guests essentially filled the resort. But for all of the wrong reasons, it would become one of the most memorable events in Ojai for years to come.

On the day of the party, one of those "normal" incredibly beautiful spring Ojai days in early May, the valley was still smothered with the intoxicating aroma of orange blossoms. It was as if angels had sprinkled a heavenly perfume from the cloudless blue sky.

Roberto was beside himself with happiness, yet a bit overwhelmed from being introduced to all of the guests. Though gifted with a powerful memory, he finally gave up trying to remember all of the names. He did, however, enjoy introducing Sally and me to his friends from abroad. After much eating and dancing, the three of us were exhausted.

Following a sumptuous five-course Italian dinner, the band leader introduced Mr. Paradiso who eloquently recognized

Roberto, and expressed for both his wife and himself, how proud they were of his academic accomplishments and his warmth and love of life. And although it was not in their normal family culture to give each other extravagant gifts, he wanted the guests to share in the Paradiso's excitement to present Roberto with their very special present to him for his birthday.

During Mr. Paradiso's comments, several waiters distributed glasses of Dom Perignon champagne to all of the guests for a toast. They were invited outside to a large patio. Just beyond the patio, perfectly nested between two multi-centennial live oak trees, stood a 20-foot-tall red silk cloth flapping slightly in a mild breeze. Embossed across its center in sparkling gold letters were the words, "Happy 16th Birthday Roberto! We love you!" Mr. Paradiso walked to the large cloth and at the sound of heralding trumpets from the band, pulled a gold cord and exposed a brand new, white Ford Mustang convertible. The top was down and it was clearly loaded with every option offered.

Roberto was dumbfounded. He could barely speak. His eyes filled with tears as he ran and hugged his mom and dad. Mr. Paradiso finished with, "Roberto, we love you very much, and we felt that since the driving age in California is 16, and you've got your license, you should have your own set of wheels too!"

Sally and I were so excited for Roberto. The three of us jumped into the car, Roberto as driver, Sally in the passenger's seat, and I reeling up and down in the back seat. We were like three five-year-olds enjoying Roberto's incredible gift.

"Hey girls, let's go for a spin! What do you say?"

Sally and I responded in perfect unison, "Yes!"

"Mom, Dad, would it be alright if we go for a short spin? We'll only be about 30 minutes or so."

"Okay, son, but please drive carefully."

"Promise!"

With that, the three of us snapped on our seat belts and we were off, serenaded by the applause of all the guests.

※

Roberto drove west through town on Ojai Avenue, which runs into Highway 150 and up into the mountains towards Santa Paula. It was dark but clear as a bell. The Milky Way looked like a bright heavenly chandelier stretched across the sky.

"Look guys, our beautiful Milky Way!" I exclaimed. One of the magnificent benefits of the Ojai Valley was the absence of light pollution, so the dramatic glow of the Milky Way galaxy was not an uncommon occurrence.

"You girls go ahead and look but I need to take these winding curves as carefully as possible. I'm telling you though, this car almost drives itself."

"It's a real beauty, Roberto. Sandra and I are so happy for you!"

"You bet, Roberto; just as long as we remain your BFFs (Best Friends Forever)! Only kidding!"

"I know, Sandra. Look, you both have played an import part in my life over the past few years. It's been great, and it will continue to be great. I'm absolutely sure!"

Always the concerned and sensitive one among the three of us, Sally quizzed, "Hey, don't you think we ought to get back to the party? Your folks might be concerned."

Roberto noted as they were driving past Dennison Park, "Right! It's quite dark and curvy here. In a few miles, we'll be passing Lion Canyon Reservoir. I'll turn around there and head back."

Sally was about to say something to me. As she turned around, she noticed I had removed my seatbelt and was sitting up on the rear of the back seat, my arms stretched to the heavens, staring up at the stars. I always was the risk-taker between us, sometimes very reckless risks.

"Sandra, are you crazy? Please sit down and put your seatbelt on!"

"Oh Sis, don't be so motherly. I'm getting high on the universe! The Milky Way bathed in a cool Ojai Valley breeze, scented with the aroma of orange blossoms; it's magnificent!"

Roberto jumped in. "Sandra, please do as she says or I'm going to stop the car."

"Roberto, no wonder you and Sally get along so well. You both seem to be cut from the same cloth."

At that very moment, Roberto had reached a sharp left turn just before Lion Canyon Reservoir. A pickup truck driving in the oncoming direction by 72 year old Michael Farmer started to drift into Roberto's lane. Farmer must have fallen asleep at the wheel, as it would later be learned that he had no alcohol in his bloodstream.

Roberto, driving at the speed limit, swerved to the right to avoid a head-on collision and slammed on the brakes. But he could not avoid a collision entirely. The Mustang flew into the air and then crashed its way down a steep embankment, toppling over several times before settling upside down at the bottom. Both front seat airbags inflated, however their saving grace was minimal.

Farmer unfortunately was carrying a full gallon glass jug of gasoline in his front seat. He apparently used it to power the lawn-mower that was chained in the back of his pickup. After a head-on collision with a tree, the cab of his truck burst into flames and he perished in a crematorium, hopefully not feeling any pain after hitting the tree at full force.

Fortunately for us, a young man and his wife were following not very far behind us. He immediately called 911 and the Ojai emergency squad was there in less than 10 minutes.

Because of the airbags and the safety roll bar Mr. Paradiso had installed behind the front seat, Roberto survived with a broken leg, a broken arm and two fractured ribs. Sally and I were not so lucky.

Sally had multiple contusions, a broken arm, but most seriously, a sharp tree branch had punctured her left lower abdomen and all but decimated her left and only kidney. At Ojai Valley Community Hospital, she was put on a dialysis machine as preparations were made to move her to Santa Barbara's Cottage Hospital where a renal specialist would assess her options.

I, deservedly for my stupidity, fared worst of all. At the moment of impact, having no seat belt on, I was airborne immediately and hit a large tree at only God knows how many miles-per-hour. It was enough to destroy many of the important working parts of my brain. But by some fluke (or, was it?) my respiratory system and heart survived.

I remember being mentally present in the ambulance. I could not hear, see or feel anything. Yet, although my five senses were gone, my sixth sense was still intensely present and I was aware of everything going on around me. The paramedics were working diligently and rapidly to administer life sustaining infusions into my veins and I was doing everything with my focused paranormal powers to stay present until we arrived at the hospital. I knew I would eventually have to leave my body.

In a matter of minutes we reached Ojai Valley Community Hospital. Only then did I relax my focus and immediately shut down. I was put on total ventilation to keep my vegetative body "alive" until Mom and Dad could decide what to do. A difficult decision had to be made.

No matter how often it happens in our world, it is always terribly sad and difficult to fathom how so many lives can in just a single instant be inflicted with guilt, anger, regret, heart-brake and despondency. It's due in part to our deep attachment to our loved ones and in part to our clinging to our perception of the impermanence of life. It is nearly impossible for most of us to accept philosopher Pierre Teilhard de Chardin's personal conviction that *We are not human beings having a spiritual experience. We are spiritual beings having a human experience*—sometimes a brief one at that.

The accident brought Mom and Dad and Isabella and Mario Paradiso close together. They cried, prayed and suffered as one, but this did not lessen the weight of the pain they carried for themselves and for each other. This, of course, was an especially tragic time for Mom and Dad.

It was three days after the accident and Dr. Patton, a renal specialist at Cottage Hospital, completed his analysis of Sally's condition. He was meeting with Mom and Dad to explain options they could choose from for Sally's and my future. They were in one of the hospital conference rooms for more than an hour.

When they exited, both Mom and Dad were deeply distraught and in tears. Isabella and Mario ran to them and embraced them both. None of them could speak for several minutes, then Mom did the best she could to explain Dr. Patton's conclusions. Dad had moved to a nearby chair, bent forward with his face buried in his hands.

"Sally's only kidney is badly damaged from a puncture wound by a tree branch. It cannot be saved…She will have to spend the rest of her life on dialysis, and it will very likely be a short life."

Isabella offered empathy. "Margaret, with all of the modern technology, isn't there something they can do beyond that?"

"Yes, but the risks are very high."

Dad stood up, his eyes red and bleary from crying. "There is one thing they can do, but it will destroy our family."

Mario held Dad in his arms. "Mio amigo, please, what is that?"

Dad slowly raised his head and looked Mario in the eye. "We would have to give up Sandra." Then he sat back down and sobbed uncontrollably.

Mario, dumbfounded, stared at Mom.

"Mario, Isabella, Sandra is in a permanent vegetative state. The doctors all say that the brain damage is so severe there is absolutely no possibility of recovery, even slightly…The impact of Sandra's body with the tree was so significant that it destroyed not only her brain, but nearly all of her internal organs. Her kidneys were badly damaged. One is completely gone, but the other may possibly function if transplanted immediately to Sally and repaired during surgery. This surgery would be so traumatic for Sandra's body that it would end her life. Even if she lived, she would remain in a vegetative state with no kidneys and on permanent dialysis.

"In any case, regardless of whether we choose to do this or not, the doctors are advising us to consider shutting down all of the machines that keep her alive. Alternatively, they could put Sally's name on a kidney transplant list, but there is no guarantee as to if and when she would get a donor match. Sandra, of course, as an identical twin is a perfect donor. There would be no risk of future complications, *if* they succeeded in repairing her damaged kidney. And that's a big *if*. We need to make the decision by tomorrow morning to have the best chance of success for a successful transplant to Sally, if that is the direction we choose."

Mario convinced Mom and Dad to return to the Ojai Valley Inn with him and Isabella. He had a suite prepared for them so they would not have to be alone that evening. They needed to rest well before making one of the most important decisions of their lives...

As I lay in my bed at Cottage Hospital with all of the physical stillness you would expect in a closed-in vegetative state, my spirit, my true *Self* was quite alive and active. Even with the distance between us, I could clearly sense Mom and Dad's unbearable stress. *But how was that possible?*

Although I had heard the reason many times from Masters Ben and Dam, I knew in that moment the answer to be a universal truth. Your spirit, your soul, or whatever you wish to call it, is eternal. It is your true *Self*, and it never dies. Your *Self* is your eternal consciousness and *it* creates your mind, not the converse. That's why when your mind or brain is gone, your *Self*, or what Eastern Wisdom calls your *I Am*, is ever-present and can tune in to other thought patterns.

As my body lay in bed, I focused all of my spiritual energy on Mom and Dad's spirits and assured them that giving my kidney to Sally was the absolute moral thing to do. In the end, they would find it best for all of us. I knew quite well they would not see this point clearly that evening, but I also knew they most definitely would in the not-too-distant future.

Dr. Patton was in his office at 7:00 the next morning waiting for Mom and Dad to arrive at 8:00 am. Today was an early arrival for him. He wanted to think about what to say should they decide not to proceed with the kidney transplant. Although he had witnessed numerous difficult patient decisions during the course of his career, this was unquestionably the most challenging he had ever encountered. A physician was supposed to remain emotionally uninvolved, but Dr. Patton could feel Mom and Dad's pain.

The Paradisos drove my parents to Cottage Hospital, and they arrived in Dr. Patton's office a bit before 8:00.

"Good morning Mr. and Mrs. Brunel, please come in." They sat in chairs across from Dr. Patton.

Dad, who was normally the first to speak, was quiet and detached. Mom spoke up.

"Doctor, I will make this brief. Alan and I have gone over this decision numerous times. As you might imagine, it has been very difficult for us. But after considerable thought, we have decided to give Sandra's functioning kidney to Sally. What do you feel are the odds that this damaged kidney will actually recover after you do what you can to repair it?"

"Mrs. Brunel, I can make no promises. All I can say is that I will do my utmost best. Yesterday, I consulted with other renal experts at Harvard and UCLA Medical Schools. They are optimistic as am I, but calculating probabilities for procedures such as this one is well beyond our current medical knowledge."

Dad finally contributed, "Honey, let's just do it."

"Okay doctor … Alan and I agree. How should we proceed?"

"I have instructed ER to be on call and prep for surgery. Two assisting surgeons have also been notified and are prepared for the surgery. We have all of the pre-op tests done, so we can wheel Sally and Sandra into the ER in about 30 minutes. The entire process will take about six to eight hours.

"Normally, a transplant would take about three hours. However, we have to do quite a bit of microsurgery to repair Sandra's kidney before it is transplanted. After the repairs, we will place her kidney in Sally's abdomen. Because she has only one kidney there is lots of room. That makes things a bit easier. Then blood vessels from Sandra's repaired kidney will be connected to arteries and veins in Sally's abdomen, and the ureter from Sandra's kidney will be connected to Sally's bladder."

"Doctor, I have a request," enquired Dad.

"Yes?"

"Roberto is now allowed out of bed and can get around by wheelchair. Do you suppose we can bring him in to see Sally and Sandra before the surgery?"

"Sure, but I must caution you not to allow him to tell Sally about the outcome of this surgery. As far as she should know, Sandra is still comatose and is donating one of her kidneys. I am a big believer in going into a surgical procedure, especially one as serious as this one, with the greatest optimism the patient can muster."

Within 15 minutes, Roberto silently wheeled himself into Sally's room. I lay still and on life-sustaining technology in the adjacent room. I still had a modest level of paranormal sensing, so I was aware of what was happening around me. The hypnotic cadence of the machines attached to my body was apparent to anyone in either of the rooms as the door connecting the two rooms remained open. Roberto had been informed of what was about to take place and was using all of the emotional and spiritual energy he could conjure up to remain as calm as possible. As he sat beside Sally, she opened her eyes. Despite her current condition, she was almost her usual humorous self.

"Hi Roberto; wow what a mess you are! Are you here for some sympathy, you crazy Italian superstar?"

"No Sally, I just wanted to check in with you and see how you are doing."

"Well, it looks like not as well as you, but a lot better than Sandra. Apparently, the doctors induced an artificial coma to help her heal. I hear they will be waking her up tomorrow or the next day after good ole' Sis donates one of her two good kidneys to me. She's a real hero." Sally had absolutely no idea of Sandra's condition.

"Right."

"Roberto, your eyes are so red and bloodshot. Have you been crying?"

"No, it's a terrible cold I contracted a couple of days ago. You know hospitals!"

"Sure do, and I can't wait to get out of here even though I must admit the service here is pretty darn good. It looks like Sandra and I will only be here for a week or so after surgery. What about you?"

Roberto was quiet for several seconds. He was struggling to maintain his composure. His thoughts were of Sally, and in particular of me knowing I would never be part of their trio again—ever. He was an emotional Italian boy and desperately needed to relieve the pressure in his soul with an uncontrolled cry, and to hug Sally. But he couldn't. He needed to be strong for her. "Sally, you and Sandra have a big day ahead you. I'm going to be sending positive energy to you both until we are together again later in the recovery room."

With that, he leaned forward as she moved her head to the edge of the bed and gave her a gentle kiss on her forehead. "I think I'll stop by next door and wish Sandra the same."

"Be sure to give her a good luck kiss too."

"I promise."

With that he slowly navigated the toggle drive on the electric wheelchair with his good arm, and moved slowly through the connecting door to my room. Roberto was there for only a couple of minutes. I'm sure that was all he could bare.

All Sally could here from her bed was, "Sandra, I am praying for you. What an incredible gift you are giving to Sally. God bless you."

And then he kissed the side of my face. It was the first time he had ever kissed me. I will remember it forever.

Roberto then slowly moved toward the door to exit my room. And I was glad; had he stayed just a few seconds more he would have seen the tears rolling down the side of my face. He did not dare go back through Sally's room. I could feel his sorrow from him seeing me like that was so deep; it was cutting to his very core and vehemently attacking his composure. As he approached the door in my room, he uncontrollably released a sorrowful groan, then immediately heard Sally's call from the other room.

"Roberto, are you alright?"

With his back to her, he took several beats to reach a modicum of composure.

"Oh Sally, this darn cold; I'm going to ask my doctor for some antihistamines. Love you Sally. Love you Sandra. Gotta go. See you guys later."

And with that, Roberto pushed the toggle into fast mode and exited the room before Sally could ask another questions. When he was well into the hallway, Roberto put his face into the hand of his good arm and wept like never before in his life. My soul could feel his pain; and I wept too, but thankfully, there was no one there to see me.

However, I was also truly happy for Sally and Roberto. I had not the slightest bit of fear. For the first time in my short life, I felt a deep sense of ultimate freedom and total peace. Yes, it did come at the ultimate price, but it was so worth it.

Mr. Paradiso came to the wheelchair, knelt before Roberto and held him tightly as all present in the hallway looked on with empathy and compassion. Even strangers who knew nothing of what was happening could feel Roberto's pain. We truly are all connected.

CHAPTER 13
ACCEPTANCE

*"Understanding is the first step to acceptance, and
only with acceptance can there be recovery."*
—J. K. Rowling

It was two weeks before Sally would have more than a few words of conversation with anyone. Learning of my death and the details surrounding it was more than she could deal with. She had not been well enough to attend my funeral at Santa Barbara Cemetery, one of the most beautiful in California, resting high on a bluff overlooking the Pacific Ocean. Roberto had the services videotaped, and one day he would show the film to Sally. After a beautiful and loving eulogy by Roberto, half of my ashes were maintained at the cemetery and the other half solemnly dispersed into the Pacific as a flock of white doves were released to a heavenly blue sky. I could see that everyone there felt my presence.

Sally still spent some of her days in bed as the repaired kidney healed and began to function normally. Roberto visited, but his stays were short. He mainly held her hand and talked about inconsequential happenings in Ojai. Summer was nearly over and the two of them would soon be heading back to the Wisdom Academy though Sally showed no signs of interest in going back to school.

Roberto finally decided it was time to address the issues that were hanging over both of them. Mom and Dad had tried, but it always ended in uncontrollable tears among all of them. As he drove back to Ojai one Friday afternoon, he had an idea. On his way to Santa Barbara that morning, he had noticed a sign that said the Humane Society of Ventura County was having a pet adoption event on Saturday. He decided to visit and see if he could find a cute and playful puppy for Sally. *This just might be the thing to start her emotional healing process.*

The next morning, as he drove down Bryant Street in Ojai where the Humane Society had its main office and facilities, he saw quite a few people gathering to inspect the available pets. Immediately upon arriving, Roberto found a large number of cyclone-fence cages housing dogs of all sizes. There were a few horses on site and several cats too. Roberto was partial to dogs though. He was going to look for a beautiful small puppy, perhaps a terrier, one that Sally could easily play with in the house.

As he moved from cage to cage, he started to rate his top three choices that would then lead to his final decision. As he did this, a Maine Coon kitten kept lurching at his pants leg. He consistently wiggled the kitten off. A young lady who was one of the workers noticed Roberto and came over to speak with him.

"I see that our little Maine Coon kitten has a thing for you!"

"I guess so; he or she, whichever, won't let me peacefully choose a puppy."

"Well, it's a 'she,' and she is so athletic, she just won't stay in her cage. She wandered in here last week. But the weird thing is that every time someone shows an interest in taking her, she roars and hisses disapproval at them. You're the only one she has shown any affection for. Amazing!"

Roberto picked up the kitten and stared into her crystal clear green eyes, the same color as the twins. She stared back with an intent and affection that was surreal.

"You're a beauty, little guy, I mean gal. What's your name?"

"We haven't had time to give her one. Are you interested in taking her?"

Roberto had his heart set on a puppy, but there was something magical about this little kitten. "I need a pet for a good friend who is recovering from a terrible trauma. I was thinking of a puppy."

"I know who you are," said the young lady. "You're the boy who was involved in that terrible accident a few months ago up on Route 150. It was all over the local papers. I'm so sorry for you and your friends, the twins, oh dear lord."

"Thank you." Roberto stood quietly for a long two beats. "Okay, I tell you what. I will take the kitten, but if she doesn't work out for my friend Sally, I will need to bring her back to you. Is that acceptable?"

"Absolutely!"

And with that, Roberto took the little kitten in a small cage he borrowed from the center for transport to Sally's home. He bought a soft kitty bed and a load of food and snacks. He wondered if he was doing the right thing. He would soon find out. He was on his way to visit Sally in Santa Barbara.

Roberto had his arms full of kitty stuff as he fumbled to ring the bell at our home. Mom answered.

"Hi there Roberto! My lord, what's all this? Roberto stared at Mom somewhat bewildered. Within a few seconds, all was clear. "My goodness, you've gotten Sally a kitten. How sweet of you!"

"Well, I don't know about that. We'll have to see how she responds to this little critter. I got her at the Ventura Humane Society in Ojai. She was running wild in their yard. The interesting thing is that she didn't seem to want to be with anyone there but me. Now that's weird!"

With that, the kitten started meowing at Mom. "Wow, she likes you too Mrs. Brunel!"

"You're a lovely little kitten. You know Roberto, I think she's gonna fit right in. Come on in. Sally's upstairs. She just got out of the shower. Just give her a few minutes before you go up to her room."

"Mrs. Brunel, has there been any change?"

"Not really. Alan and I are thinking of asking her to see a psychological counselor. We just don't know what to do. It's been nearly two and half months and school starts in a couple of weeks. She can't go to school in this condition."

"I understand. If there is anything I or my family can do, please let me know."

"I will, I will, Roberto. Why don't you go up and surprise her with the kitten. I'll be bringing up her breakfast in a few minutes."

"Okay, thanks."

Roberto climbed the stairs with the little kitten resting comfortably in the travel cage. He placed the cage just before the entrance to Sally's room and then made his appearance.

"Hi Sally!"

"Oh, hi there Roberto."

"What you been doing since yesterday?"

"Oh the usual, just hanging around. Mom keeps reminding me that school starts soon. I'm dreading going back."

"And why is that?"

"For a couple of reasons; I don't want to be constantly reminded with thoughts of sympathy about Sandra, but most important, I am going to be constantly depressed by the loss of our..." Sally started to cry and barely pronounced the last two words... "Dy...nam...ic... trio."

Roberto ran to the side of her bed and held her for several moments until she could regain a level of composure.

"Look Sally; we'll get through this together. I'll be there with you, and we have all of the support of our classmates, our teachers, Masters Dam and Ben, Joon, your parents, mine...it'll work out, I promise. And to get your mind going in hopefully a better direction, I have a surprise for you."

"What?"

At that very moment, the kitten let out just the slightest "meow."

"What was that?"

"What was what?"

"That sound!"

"I didn't hear anything."

"Roberto, are you sure?"

"I'm sure, but let me look around."

As Sally watched inquisitively, Roberto looked in the closet, under the bed, and then sauntered slowly to the door and peeked around the entrance to Sally's room.

"Well, what is this?" as he picked up the small cage and carried it slowly to Sally's bed where she sat upright in anticipation of what Roberto had in his hands. He laid it down, the cage opening facing Sally."

"Oh my God! Roberto, she's so cute!"

"How did you know it's a she?"

"I just do."

Sally opened the cage and the kitten immediately ran up Sally's pajamas and began licking her, kissing her, all over her face.

"She is so adorable, and so friendly!"

"That's what you think! She was hissing and scratching at everyone who came near her at the Humane Society. You, your Mom and I are the only ones she would even come close to. It's amazing!"

Just then Mom and Dad entered the room with Sally's breakfast.

"Oh Sally, what a cutie! What about a name?" Mom asked.

Sally closed her eyes and thought for a few seconds.

"Sandra. Her name is Sandra."

Roberto, Mom and Dad didn't say a word. The sensitivity of this subject was beyond anyone's comprehension and certainly not open for discussion. But then, in a mysterious moment of unison, the three of them noticed more than a semblance of joy on Sally's face. They weren't sure why, it was only a little kitten, but they didn't care why. They hadn't seen this sign of love and beauty on Sally's face for months since the accident.

Mom and Dad rushed to Sally's bed and sat opposite Roberto.

"Sally, Mom and I are so very happy for you and *Sandra*. Roberto, you could not have chosen a better present for Sally, no, for all of us! Thank you son!"

Little Sandra had taken a rest from licking Sally and ran across her bed to Mom and Dad, taking turns snuggling next to each of them. This was a magical moment for all four, no all *five* of them.

The conversation began to flow as it did before the accident, and there were smiles on all faces in the room, most especially Sally's. Then in a flash, Sandra jumped off the bed and began to strut like a mini-tiger for the door. Sally called out as if she were speaking to her sister, "Now Sandra, where do you think you are you going?"

At that very instant, kitty Sandra stopped, paused, and then turned only her head back and looked straight into Sally's eyes. Mom, Dad and Roberto were mystified. But Sally wasn't. She sensed something special in Sandra. Actually, she knew quite well what it was.

"Sandra, will you please come back here? I love you! We love you!"

And with that, Sandra turned and scampered back and in a flying leap landed in Sally's arms.

Mom, Dad and Roberto were speechless. They stared alternately at each other, but it was only several seconds before their eyes began to well-up with tears of joy.

How could this possibly be? It didn't matter. All that mattered was that it was.

EPILOGUE

*"Waking up to who you really are requires letting
go of who you imagine yourself to be."*
—Alan Watts

This has been my story—so far—written accurately and dispassionately, directly from the Akashic Records. And the
Akashic Records are never in error, they are always the absolute
truth. It was a 16-year journey of trial and error that ushered me
though a chaotic arc from the *Bad Seed* through redemption,
and finally to deep appreciation for the value and power of love
among family and friends. I wish it could have been a longer
period of time so that I could have done much more for Sally,
Roberto, Mom and Dad—for the world. But the Universe knows
better than I. And perfect evolution of the *Oneness* of *Universal
Consciousness* is the name of the Cosmic game; it takes total
precedence.

In the spirit of our connected consciousness, I would like to
share several poignant lessons I learned during my journey on
earth and as a consequence of "crossing over." I offer them for your
consideration and hopefully, for your benefit. You certainly don't
have to believe them, unless any of them ring true for you.

As many who have had near-death experiences and subsequently
described them in some detail, it's true, you do encounter a bright
white light as you navigate a tunnel filled with images of people
who have passed on before you. But, this may well be hardwired
into our brains culturally, as there is no continuous physical image

contact or "normal" communication with those who died before you. However, you do feel their presence and spiritual communication, and there is an intense presence of unbounded knowledge, wellbeing and happiness—all beyond human verbal expression.

There is no God in the forms created by men over the ages, no wise all-powerful being with a white beard managing creation. Instead, you become intimately aware of an infinitely intelligent mind that has always been and always will be—and you are an intimate and integral part of that mind. You can certainly call this God, or perhaps *Cosmic Consciousness* (my preference), or any of a host of other earthly labels. The name is irrelevant, except if it implies ineffective and false ideas within your mindset.

One of my more compelling findings is that *the only purpose of all material creation, including you and me, is to provide a mechanism for Cosmic Consciousness to become increasingly aware of itself.* Yes, *Cosmic Consciousness* is perfect in every way, but it cannot be aware of, or experience itself without the presence of material creation looking back at it. *That is how critically important we are* to the continuous and infinite evolution of all present in *Universal Consciousness* towards total and complete *Oneness!*

Time and space do not exist after death in the world of spirit. These are human constructs to manage and explain material existence. However, in earthly language, some "half of infinity" ago, *Cosmic Consciousness* decided to move to this mode of existence as a means to become increasingly aware of its *Self.* And this will go on forever as the Universe, over trillions of years, expands and then contracts back to the singularity from which it was birthed. This cyclical process of birth and death of the Universe is set to continue for all eternity. As a consequence, all material things, especially sentient beings, will continue to evolve in consciousness towards perfect *Oneness.*

As a result of my brief experience as Sandra Brunel, I have learned that we truly are all connected at the level of spirit, and what deeds anyone does affects not only themselves, but all other beings as well. That's why my actions affected my family and friends, and as I have now learned, even beyond them. They suffered with me and for me.

I want you to know that *Karma* is alive and well. It is not a form of reward or punishment. It simply means, just as Isaac Newton taught us about the world of physical mechanics, *every action has an equal and opposites reaction*. We must get our spiritual lives in perfect perpetual alignment to reach what some have called *enlightenment*. And if we don't do so during a given lifetime, we have the opportunity to return to the material world time and again to eventually get it right. Yes, *reincarnation* is a powerful and effective tool for us as well.

Therefore, since your spirit and the evolution of consciousness are both eternal, you can choose when and how you return to the material world to set things in the right direction. I think by now, if you have read "between the lines," you are well aware of what my choice was. You see, I desperately wanted to set things right with Sally and Roberto, and with Mom and Dad. So far, so good! Life is truly beautiful!

Wishing you great success and fulfillment as you travel your chosen path,

Sandra

About the Author

James A. Cusumano (www.JamesCusumano.Com) is chairman and owner of Chateau Mcely (www.chateaumcely.cz/en/homepage), chosen in 2007 by the European Union as the only "Green" 5-star, castle hotel in Central Europe, and in 2008 by the World Travel Awards as *The World's Leading Green Hotel*. Chateau Mcely offers programs that promote the principles of Inspired and Conscious Leadership, finding your Life Purpose and Long-Term Fulfillment.

He began his career during the 1950s in the field of entertainment as a recording artist. Years later, after a PhD in physical chemistry, business studies at Harvard and Stanford and as a Foreign Fellow of Churchill College at Cambridge University, he joined Exxon as a research scientist and later became their research director for Catalytic Science & Technology.

Dr. Cusumano subsequently cofounded two public companies in Silicon Valley, Catalytica Energy Systems, Inc.—devoted to clean power generation; and Catalytica Pharmaceuticals, Inc., which manufactured drugs via environmentally-benign, low-cost, catalytic technologies. While he was chairman and CEO, Catalytica Pharmaceuticals grew in less than five years, from several employees to 2,000 and became more than a $1 billion enterprise before being sold.

Subsequent to his work in Silicon Valley and before buying and renovating Chateau Mcely with his wife Inez, Dr. Cusumano returned to entertainment and founded Chateau Wally Films (www.chateauwallyfilms.biz), which produced the feature film *What*

Matters Most (2001: www.imdb.com/title/tt0266041), distributed in more than 50 countries.

He is the coauthor of *Freedom from Mid-East Oil* (2007), and author of *Cosmic Consciousness – A Journey to Well-being, Happiness and Success* (2011), *BALANCE: The Business—Life Connection* (2013), *Life Is Beautiful: 12 Universal Rules* (2016) and *The Fallen: A Thriller from the World of Consciousness* (2016).

Dr. Cusumano lives in Prague with his wife, Inez, and their daughter, Julia.

www.ingramcontent.com/pod-product-compliance
Lightning Source LLC
Chambersburg PA
CBHW071335130626
46556CB00004B/1908